CW00727415

They sat on the ~~~~~~~~~~~~~~~~~~~~ ~~~ were
at least six atten~~~~~~~~~~~~~~~ right. Ramzana
read out the final ~~~~~~

Dear Mr Underhill, MP
We are two boys who are fighting hard . . .'

Brendan interrupted. 'He might think we were fighting,'
he objected. 'I mean the two of us . . .'

'Listen to what comes next,' Ramzana replied.
'Fighting hard *to* save a meadow. Not just fighting.'

'All right then,' agreed Brendan. It was of paramount
importance that this first move should be flawless.

STILL WATERS

Pratima Mitchell

RED FOX

A Red Fox Book
Published by Random House Children's Books
20 Vauxhall Bridge Road, London SW1V 2SA

A division of Random House UK Ltd
London Melbourne Sydney Auckland
Johannesburg and agencies throughout the world

First published in 1992 by The Bodley Head Children's Books

Red Fox edition 1994

3 5 7 9 10 8 6 4 2

© Pratima Mitchell 1992

The right of Pratima Mitchell to be identified as the
author of this work has been asserted by her in
accordance with the Copyright, Designs and Patents
Act, 1988

This book is sold subject to the condition that it shall
not, by way of trade or otherwise, be lent, resold, hired
out, or otherwise circulated without the publisher's
prior consent in any form of binding or cover other
than that in which it is published and without a similar
condition including this condition being imposed on
the subsequent purchaser

Printed and bound in Great Britain by
Cox & Wyman Ltd, Reading, Berkshire

RANDOM HOUSE UK Limited Reg. No. 954009

ISBN 0 09 999790 8

*For Shakuntala Bhatia
and Priya*

1

Friday evening, the best time of the week. Night falling soft as an eiderdown on the canal. Brendan lies on his stomach, eyeball to eyeball with a potato-peel, carpet fluff and a teaspoon lurking under the bookcase.

He pulls down another *Rupert Bear Annual* from a stack on the bottom shelf, slapping it on the floor with unnecessary energy, crack! An exasperated grunt-cum-sigh whooshes from the direction of the kitchen table. All evening, he's been trying, almost unconsciously, to annoy Will, his stepfather, but there hasn't yet been a confrontation.

He turns his attention to *Rupert*. All the annuals once belonged to his mother, and *Clara Strong* is written on the title pages in an upright, slightly wobbly script. The pages are well-thumbed from Clara's hands when she was young. Brendan reads them over and over again. They link him to his mother's childhood and also because in some strange way he identifies with Rupert. Rupert is gallant and clever. Eager, bright-eyed, chivalrous boy-bear, he shuttles from one adventure to the next. His is a world of familiar and exotic landscapes, full of friends, atmosphere and magic. Myth and reality. In Brendan's opinion Tin-Tin and Asterix aren't a patch on Rupert.

Harried or in trouble, Rupert is always capable and in control, a leader.

Brendan never reads anything else, except when he has to, at school. Boring old reading-scheme books. The text in the annuals rhymes, the pictures are brilliant, the stories bowl along. Once, soon after his marriage to his mother, Will had invited him to go with him to the library, but Brendan had shown no enthusiasm. It was clear that there were parts of himself he didn't want to share.

While Brendan reads, his long brown hair flopping over his eyes, Will does his accounts and Clara sews. She is in her rocking chair, bent over her embroidery, silk-threads all over her jumper. She pricks the taut cloth in the frame with a precise, downward movement of her needle. Then out it comes again. In and out. She is making an embroidery picture on commission. Rolling grey hills, fluffily clouded skies, blue river, a tree fruiting paradisal apples. She also paints canalware in the traditional way; enamel jugs, dippers, kettles and buckets festooned with cabbage roses, sunsets and castles.

A typical Friday evening. Brendan felt his eyes becoming gritty. The oil-lamps, one by Clara and one on the kitchen table, didn't carry enough light to the floor. Will needed the table for his typewriter and ledgers. Rupert was trying to rescue a princess locked up in a castle tower. Clara looked a bit like her, with her sheet of bright brown hair and her old-fashioned long skirt. No, she was more like a painting he'd seen on a class visit to the museum last week.

They were 'doing' the Victorians. 'Very sentimental,' Mr Bulmer had pronounced. 'Soupy emotionalism and melodrama. Nice colours, though. This was a very famous group of Victorian painters,' he said, waving his hand at a wall of paintings. 'Called themselves the Pre-Raphaelites.' Simon Thripp and Tariq had clowned around as usual, simpering and clasping their hands to their chests, falling on their knees and rolling their eyes piously to the ceiling. But Brendan had looked for a long time at a Burne-Jones picture of Guinevere and Lancelot. She reminded him of Clara with her great, sad eyes. But if Clara looked like Queen Guinevere, Will had nothing in common with Sir Lancelot, Sir Kay or any of Arthur's knights, thought Brendan.

Will sat wedged between the cabin wall and the table, a short fat man with unruly hair caught back in a pony-tail. Brendan stared critically at him. Beer-belly, beard, ear-ring, plaid shirt, jeans, the works. He had 'hippy' written all over him. He watched with a mixture of fascination and repulsion as he took a swig of Thornbridge Best Bitter, rubbed his eyes and burped loudly. 'Pardon,' he said with what sounded like exaggerated politeness. Out whooshed another characteristic grunt-sigh.

Worse than that teenage tennis star, Monica Seles, thought Brendan.

'What's the matter, dear? Isn't it adding up?'

'It never will. Two unpaid accounts.' Will shifted his bulk and peered short-sightedly at the ledger.

Too vain to get his eyes tested, said the auto-critic in Brendan's head. On the other hand, if he found he did need glasses he'd probably come back with coloured contact lenses, a different colour for each eye. Will liked to play up his eccentricity.

A series of jabs at the calculator. 'That's two hundred and eighty pounds still owing from those Christmas weddings. Why will they get married in the sleet and snow if they're not prepared to pay for the pleasure? Third reminder.'

He inserted a piece of paper in the machine with the heading:

William Dangerfield
Old Tyme Weddings
Let us transport you to the church on time

He started clattering away in a professional manner.

Running after money, thought Brendan, and calls himself a Marxist.

He hadn't always felt the need to demolish Will. They'd got along just fine when he'd been Clara's gentleman-caller, as she had described him to her mother on the telephone.

'Oh Mum, he's making kitchen shelves for me. Yes, all right he's got a thing about me, but he isn't my *boyfriend*. . .' she giggled, 'he's a gentleman caller.' Then she'd noticed Brendan listening from his bedroom and winked naughtily at him.

'Anyway, I don't think Brendan would approve, would you love?' she'd added, throwing him a bright glance which had erased all the sadness from her face. But Brendan wasn't completely reassured. He'd watched Will's adoring looks. If only he'd known then how he would feel about Will, now that he was a permanent fixture, he'd never have agreed to his mother marrying him he thought fiercely.

'Brendan are you sure you don't mind? Are you absolutely sure? You like him don't you?'

At that point he could quite truthfully say he did.

It had always been just him and Clara, ever since he was three and his dad had walked out on them, taking his guitar and his Leadbelly records all the way back to America, where he came from. Brendan was eleven now and starting to get curious about a bigger world than the one he had grown up in; Granny Strong, Polly in the next boat, Clara's other friends.

Will took him fishing, let him drive his pony trap, got him all excited about Friends of the Earth and saving the planet, made him feel more grown-up.

Will was a character all right. He had two lines of work: he made kitchen fittings for Wilson's the builders and he hired out a beautiful little bottle-green and gold pony trap for weddings and highdays. At those times he transformed himself into a distinguished-looking figure dressed in knee breeches, white stockings, waistcoat and tails and a jaunty top hat. He'd taken Brendan along a few times on these occasions to hold the ponies. Brendan had been overjoyed with the £5 tips that came his way without much effort.

He had liked Will. Funny how quickly things had changed once he moved in with them. It was really hard getting used to another body on *Fair Rosamund*. Will was large and he was untidy. He dropped his clothes where he took them off, Clara was always fishing out socks and Y-fronts from all sorts of places. Clara, who'd kept such a neat-as-a-pin boat, who used to nag Brendan if he didn't stow away everything, hardly ever said a word. Mysteriously, the rules were different for Will. It wasn't exactly *betrayal*, Brendan had thought, just that Clara didn't have to be so accommodating. She was happy and that hurt in a strange way. And his burps and belches and the way he dribbled spag bol down his beard – Brendan gave an inward shudder and turned a page.

A piece of paper was stuck in it, like a bookmark. He remembered he'd copied out an ad from the window of Mr Khan's newspaper shop. 'Sony colour TV for sale.

5

Owner going abroad, reasonable price.' He grinned, folded it into a paper dart and flicked it at Will. It hit him on his nose as he was concentrating on getting the right kind of iron-fist-in-a-velvet-glove effect.

'Yargh,' he grunted, 'what the. . . ?' The dart fell on the keyboard. Will looked distinctly peeved. He unfolded it, read it and said in an infinitely patient voice, 'Brendan, we've had this out before and the answer is still no.' And smiling sweetly, he continued typing.

Brendan felt a tightness in his chest and an oceanic, roaring anger in his head. A confused mixture of hurt pride, deflation, disappointment and sheer dislike suddenly boiled over and exploded into a shameful tantrum, like he hadn't had since he was four years old.

'I hate you, I hate you.' The other words luckily were lost in his noisy sobs. 'Go away you great, fat, ugly . . . monster!'

'Shut up!' roared the monster from his vantage point. 'Shut up and grow up. We are not, I repeat *never*, going to get a television!'

Clara snipped a thread with her teeth. Her big brown eyes were wide with shock and Brendan, through his own angry sobs, saw a tear glistening in them. The belly of the boat rocked ever so slightly under him.

The tension was unbearable. Brendan sniffed loudly and wiped his nose with his cuff. Clara bowed her head low, sewing steadily. Will chewed the end of his pencil, his eyebrows knitting together. Suddenly a high-pitched whistle splintered the silence outside.

A series of whistles and a voice calling over and over again. Spooky and most unusual for the normally peaceful colony of boats on that part of the canal.

The quarrel shelved, all three of them looked at

6

each other with some alarm and listened attentively. Will squeezed out, parted the curtains on a starboard window and peered outside. He sounded quite normal again, saying, 'Someone seems to be looking for a lost animal out there.'

The whistling came nearer, it was piercingly loud now and they could hear other sounds on the towpath, on what sounded like the other side of the liftbridge. Gravel scraping, crashing noises in the bushes and someone calling something like, 'hoash, hoash, hoash,' in a high-pitched voice.

Brendan sat up stiffly, put his annual away on its shelf and pushed open the little doors that led to the foredeck. He stepped out. It was a clear night with strongly inked shadows and a round moon, hard and bright like a headlamp. He could just make out a dark shape on the other side of the canal, moving about in the hawthorn bushes. Torch light flickered in the undergrowth.

'Ahoy! Do you need some help?' he shouted.

The dark shape straightened up, not very tall, and a boy's voice answered.

'I'm looking for a dog. Have you seen him, he's a greyhound.' The voice was vaguely familiar, the accent foreign sounding.

'Come on over. Just walk over the bridge. I'll get a light.'

Will's woolly head appeared in the little doorway. He ducked back in again and came outside with a hurricane lamp which he held high up to guide the boy as he came clattering over to their side.

Brendan found himself staring into a pair of blue-grey eyes fringed with thick black lashes under straight, very black eyebrows set in a pale face, topped by a shock of dark hair.

7

'It's Ramzana, from my class. He's a new boy.' He turned to Will, not knowing what to do.

Will took charge of the situation. 'You'd better come on board, Ramzana, and tell us what's going on. Come on in.' He was friendly and encouraging.

The boy stepped over the side, down the three steps and entered the cabin. He had on a dusty blue anorak with a ratty, fur-lined hood which exuded a rather unpleasant odour. He was as tight and tense as a coiled spring. His ears, big and reddened by the cold air, stuck out of the side of his head like goblin's wings. It seemed very bright inside, after the shadows of the night. Ramzana blinked. The polished horse-brasses, the shiny pine table, the varnished wood ceiling, the yellow metal fittings struck points of light everywhere. The rest was a blur of detail; small chairs with patchwork cushions, pots and pans hanging from the ceiling, the black wood stove, dozens of blue and white china ornaments. An Aladdin's cave.

'Cup of tea?' Clara was filling the kettle. Her big brown eyes looked kind. They always invited confidences. She had a charming way of putting her head to one side, silently enquiring. Will was always saying he had fallen in love with that gesture. There were no sharp edges about her. Everything was soft and round and inspired trust.

'I'm looking for a dog called Sultan. It's m-my u-uncle's. It r-ran away this m-morning.' Ramzana stuttered slightly as if he were very nervous. It was quite hard to follow what he said, what with the stutter and the way the words tumbled out so it seemed as though he was stumbling and running to try and catch them.

'Sit down son. Have some tea first.' Will offered him a chair. Brendan gave him a steaming mug into which

8

he'd stirred four sugars. He'd heard that lots of sugar was good for shock. Not that Ramzana was strictly in a state of shock, but he might be feeling lightheaded.

'What kind of dog is Sultan?' Clara asked.

'A greyhound. My uncle, Bashir Chacha, has two. Tipoo and Sultan. He races them but they always come last.'

Everyone laughed and it seemed to break the ice.

Brendan remembered the new boy arriving in the middle of the school year. New children were always turning up at school at odd times. He knew how they must feel, outsiders like he was; hovering on the edge of things, not belonging. Sometimes they had come from abroad and knew only a very little English. But Ramzana – in spite of his accent, rather lilting with flattened a's and extra vowels all over the place – spoke and understood it well. He even understood Mr Bulmer's peculiar sense of humour. All Brendan knew about him was that he was really keen on cricket.

Clara was muttering to herself. 'Tipoo . . . Sultan . . . Where have I heard those names before?' She rummaged in a drawer and took out a catalogue. *The Indian Exhibition at the Victoria and Albert.* She flicked through it.

'Here we are,' she read, '"Tipoo Sultan's Tiger. An amazing mechanical, life-size toy. When wound up, the tiger savages a British soldier."' She closed the catalogue. 'I saw this last month. It's three hundred years old and really sinister.'

Ramzana took a big gulp of tea.

'Is your family from India?' she asked him. He shook his head. 'From Kashmir. But I'm half English.'

'How did you lose Sultan?' asked Brendan.

'Bashir Chacha took it for a walk along that path,' he said, with a jerk of his head, 'and Sultan slipped his leash and ran away.' His arm shot forward like a plane taking off diagonally towards the ceiling, nearly knocking his mug of tea on to Will's papers.

'I haven't seen any greyhounds,' Clara said, shaking her head. 'Have you two? Polly might know something.'

'Too late to ask.' Will looked at the brass ship's clock. It was half-past ten.

'Come back tomorrow Ramzana. We'll go round and ask the other boat people and have a look on the Meadow.'

Ramzana nodded vigorously. He had a little colour in his face now. His bright blue-grey eyes, full of curiosity, roved round the cabin taking in everything.

'This where you live, then?' he asked unnecessarily.

Brendan nodded. He found it irritating that people made such a song and dance about their living on water. It made him feel even more of an oddball.

'Where do *you* live?'

'Kashmir Palace Tandoori. Upstairs.'

Clara asked, 'Don't you want to phone your mother? She must be worried about you.'

Ramzana shook his head. 'She's dead,' he said in such a matter of fact way that it could have been misunderstood as sounding casual. Brendan drew in his breath, then made out that he was sniffing. He ran the back of his hand across his nose. 'We used to live on a houseboat in Kashmir, in Srinagar, on Dal Lake. It's huge. All wooden. Four bedrooms, bathroom, sitting room, sun deck and all. We used to let out rooms to tourists, usually Germans. No, it's all right, thanks. My grandfather, Dada, won't be worried. He's the chef at the restaurant and Bashir Chacha's a waiter. They don't go to bed till one o'clock.'

Will got heavily to his feet. 'Come on then, laddie.

I'll take you back to the Kashmir Palace and you can tell us more tomorrow.'

Brendan raised a hand in salute. 'See you.'

'Bye Ramzana,' said Clara. She watched from the deck as he and Will walked to the liftbridge. Coming back in, she looked at Brendan for a minute or two.

'What was all that about, this evening Bren?' she asked sadly. 'Do you really hate Will so much? Give him a chance, and please say you're sorry when he comes back.'

He felt a sharp pang of guilt. He'd almost forgotten about the scene. He'd try and like Will again, he really would. He hated Clara being upset. But now his thoughts were full of Ramzana. He'd known nothing about him until tonight. He was half English and his mother was dead. Where was his father? He hadn't said. What was Ramzana doing with his grandfather and uncle in Stowbridge? An uncle who raced greyhounds. Where was Kashmir anyway? He'd look it up in his atlas. What must it be like living above the Kashmir Palace Tandoori? It sounded pretty amazing with no one anxious about Ramzana's whereabouts even though it was nearly eleven o'clock. He certainly was different from anyone else Brendan knew – sort of self-contained and capable. He looked as though he managed himself; dusty anorak, socks concertinaed round his ankles and the same grubby shirt he wore day in and day out. *And* he'd lived on a boat.

2

By the time Will had safely deposited Ramzana at the Kashmir Palace Tandoori it was nearly half past eleven but there were still a fair number of diners finishing their tandoori chicken and biryani after Friday night at the cinema and the pub.

Bashir gave Ramzana an enquiring look as he made out a bill. Ramzana shook his head which conveyed that his search for the dog had been fruitless. He walked into the kitchen through the swing doors. Ghulam Ali Butt, his grandfather, with thirty years' experience of cooking curries on sea and land (he'd been a ship's cook on an oil tanker) was having a last cigarette with the kitchen staff. Piles of dirty dishes and enormous pots and pans covered every available surface. All three men looked haggard and weary. They held their smokes between their third and fourth fingers, hands cupped, and drew short and hard like they would have smoked their hookahs in the old country.

'Did you find him?' asked Nasir, who was a wizard at kneading and slapping rounds of dough on the furnace-hot walls of the earthen oven to make perfectly risen bread.

'No, but I met a boy from my school. His father's going to help me look for Sultan tomorrow.'

12

Ghulam Ali ruffled his hair with his free hand and calling Ramzana by his nickname which meant 'little', said, 'It's late, Chhota. Better get to bed if you want to be on time for school.'

'It's Friday, Dada.'

'Want a game of cards, Chhota?' asked Mahmuda.

'No Mahmuda. Let him sleep now. Don't make things difficult for me. I promised Abdul Karim I would take good care of my Chhota. And now Chhota, now that your father, may Allah preserve him, has disappeared in Kashmir, my responsibility is even heavier.' Dada sounded as if he were on the verge of tears. He usually got rather sentimental at the end of a tiring day. Ramzana put his arms around him and hugged him. Dada's turmeric-stained apron smelled of the day's cooking and his henna-dyed beard tickled his cheek.

Ramzana had loved sitting on Dada's lap when he had been a small boy growing up on the lake. Dada had visited nearly every year. All day long he would sit enthroned on a Tree of Life patterned carpet on the deck, with his hookah and his cronies, playing cards and telling stories about his travels. Ramzana remembered the throaty sound of the hubble bubble; his mother Susan bringing in cups of spiced tea from the samovar, her head covered modestly in front of her father-in-law; and the ducks quacking on the water down below.

He took his grandfather's hand, brought it to his own forehead and then kissed it in a gesture of respect and farewell and went up to his room.

It was a cheerless place. Streetlight showed through the greyish nylon curtain hanging crookedly from a string stretched across the window. A couple of beds – his and his uncle's – a rickety wardrobe and a chair. That was all, except for Bashir Chacha's brand new

13

futuristic-looking music centre on which he'd blown all his savings. Ramzana got into bed and pulled a thin velvet quilt up to his chin. Even though it was so late, he didn't feel sleepy. Most nights were the same. He often lay awake until Bashir came upstairs.

He thought of Brendan's boat. He'd felt really happy for the first time since coming to England. He'd felt at home.

Susan, his mother, had run away from her family's comfortable Surrey home when she was eighteen. She hadn't really run away, she'd gone backpacking to India with a friend, but it sounded more romantic the other way. She used to tell Ramzana stories about her adventures travelling through Greece and Turkey and how she'd finally landed up in Kashmir more than 5,000 miles away from home. First she'd fallen in love with the lovely land, then met Abdul, Bashir's older brother, and fallen in love with him. She had married him and made her home in his houseboat. Then both her parents died in a car accident. After that she always said that she never wanted to go back to Surrey.

The Lady of Shalott was an old, carved cedar-wood houseboat moored next to a floating island made from tree-trunks and mud on which they grew vegetables; pale green gourds, tomatoes, beans and Kashmiri spinach, which she cooked with fiery red chillis. It was an idyllic life, especially in the summer. Every morning Ramzana would paddle his own flat-bottomed skiff, called a shikara, to the lake shore. From there he would catch a bus to school, The Tyndale Biscoe School for Boys in the Old City. He loved his school and his friends; Farid Maqbool, Riaz Muhammad, Triloke Kaul, Shyam Kak.

Then the troubles began. Something to do with politics. Loud-speakers blaring from vans day and night, riots, bombs, shooting. A kind of civil war. The Indian Army moved into Kashmir. Everything changed. Curfew at night, silent comings and goings in the houseboats, conspiracies everywhere. People they had known for years, their Hindu neighbours, silently packed up, shut their houses and shops, double-padlocked their front doors and left for the plains of India. Triloke Kaul and Shyam Kak were gone before he'd even had a chance to say goodbye to them. The school closed as one by one the teachers disappeared. The bazaars were full of rumours, the lake sinister in its unnatural silence. There was worse to come. He'd seen a dead body floating in the lake; and soldiers breaking into the fragile half-timbered waterside houses, arresting men and women and frog-marching them away with their hands behind their heads.

Ramzana would wake up in the morning, his head heavy from fearful dreams. His mouth was always dry with a tinny taste, no matter how much water or spiced tea he drank. His expectations were geared to hearing dreadful news – the worst imaginable – all the time. Of course no tourists came any more. They'd been put off by warnings of violence and kidnapping. There were no visitors at *The Lady of Shalott*, no musical evenings any more, no cheerful gossiping on the water. His father considered different plans for them. They could go to Cousin Hamid's village in the mountains, which was a safer place than Srinagar. Or Susan and Ramzana could go to England. Finally, after a lot of thought, Abdul Karim made arrangements for Susan and Ramzana to fly to England.

He bought their air tickets. He pleaded with Susan for days, but she was tearful and hysterical, refusing to leave

15

him and the house-boat. Then that dreadful thing, the worst imaginable, actually happened. One night, having cried and argued all day with Abdul Karim, Susan had an attack of her old asthma. Ramzana saw her choking and struggling for breath. Abdul Karim shouted, 'Hurry, fetch Dr Baig.'

Ramzana had run, how he had run. His heart felt that it would burst with running and with dread. The curfew was in operation and no one was allowed to go outside after dark. If the soldiers saw anyone they had orders to shoot.

Dr Baig was eating dinner. Still chewing his food, he'd pulled on his coat, grabbed his bag and followed Ramzana back to *The Lady of Shalott*.

When they got there, Ramzana saw his father sitting on the floor with Susan's head on his lap. He was weeping silently and helplessly.

Ramzana moved his head higher on the pillow. It was safe, here in his room above the restaurant. Here he could let his mind wander a little, let his thoughts linger a little. If he wanted to cry, nobody was there to see him.

A picture of grape-coloured mountains encircling the lake came before his eyes. Sounds always seemed to flee to the mountains, disappearing from the surface of the water without trace. Everyone looks at the mountains, even when there is a black storm on their summit and lightning, wicked and blue, crackles on the hill of Shankaracharya.

But now the sun is shining on *The Lady of Shalott* and the water sparkles like silvery fish-scales. Ramzana can see carp in its green depths. He won't have his bath,

16

because Susan might catch some fish in the bucket which she draws from the lake, and tip them over him. He is six years old again and she has to hold his arm in a firm grip while she soaps him without mercy from head to toe. The suds are in his eyes, he's been bitten by the carp!

'Will you stop crying. At once, do you hear? You dirty little boy. If you will play in the mud with that naughty Farida and Hamid, you'll have to have a bath every day!'

Susan is wearing a bright green *firin*, the same green as the willow trees. Her hair is caught back in a red fillet. Her turquoise and silver ear-rings dangle close to his face. Susan-bi never wears dresses or jeans. She is a Kashmiri.

'Yah, Ramzana, come and play. Yah, Ramzana, hurry Ramzana, Ramzana. . .' Voices float up to the mountains.

Now panic and darkness blotted out the friendly voices. He felt himself falling down a cliff, down the side of Shankaracharya. He shouted for help.

Bashir was sitting on his bed, looking anxiously at him.

'What's up mate? You're making a terrible racket. Having bad dreams?'

Ramzana dashed the sting of the soap suds from his eyes. His heart was racing and his forehead was covered in sweat.

He was glad his uncle had come up at last. He was only nineteen and he could always make Ramzana laugh. Bashir didn't take anything very seriously, except his young nephew and his Turkish girlfriend, Djamila. Ramzana liked her. She helped him with homework and lent him books to read. Sometimes the three of them went for walks or to the cinema.

17

Bashir asked Ramzana where he had been all evening.

'I'm going down there tomorrow to look at a boat with Djamila. We've decided to get married in the summer after her A-levels. Don't tell Dada will you?' He closed one eye and drew a finger to his lips conspiratorially. It was such a comical expression that Ramzana couldn't help smiling.

'That's better. Listen, have you heard this?' He bounced off the bed and pushed a tape into his black box, which came alive all over with little winking red lights. He kicked his legs and gyrated his boneless hips to the sound of the new Madonna. Ramzana listened for a minute or two, then snuggled deeply into his sagging bed, pulling the velvet quilt over his ears.

Brendan ambled home from the shops on Saturday afternoon, nibbling a corner of Special Organic Stone-ground bread. It was the most expensive sort, but Will had persuaded Clara it was the only kind worth ingesting. Brendan saw him from the corner of his eye, polishing the harness for a wedding. He'd tried to avoid him all morning. Will called, 'Come over a minute, Bren, I need some help.'

Brendan braced himself for the confrontation.

'Well?' Brendan forced himself to meet Will's gaze. 'Not nice,' said Will in his most disapproving tone. 'In fact, very unpleasant. I'm sorry I yelled at you, but let's not make a habit of it, eh?'

Brendan nodded.

Will was squatting on the small patch of turf by the boat. Brendan noted his fat thighs straining his jeans, his silly little Himalayan hat.

Will rubbed saddle-soap into the leather.

'Just give this a shine. Thanks. I've heard some bad

news. The paper's got a report this morning about the road on the Meadow. It's been approved by the Council.'

Brendan stopped polishing and pushed his hair impatiently back off his forehead.

Will went on, 'We've got to call an emergency committee meeting. Will you help me get it organized later today?'

He heaved himself up and slung the harness on a low alder branch, which also carried a couple of bike baskets full of clothes pegs and small gardening tools.

'There's your friend coming down the path.' Brendan followed his glance. *Friend*? That was a bit rich. He'd only known Ramzana about five minutes. Will's assumption irritated him.

'Let's get going with this dog-search, there's a lot to do tonight. Hi Ramzana, be with you in a minute,' Will called as he went to fetch his jacket.

It struck Brendan that Ramzana looked as though he had slept in his clothes. He was a bit puffy-eyed as well. But he had that self-contained, almost grown-up, air about him that he'd noticed last night.

'Sultan didn't come home then?'

'No, Bashir's gone to the Animal Sanctuary to see if he's been taken there by someone. He's coming down here later to look at a narrowboat.'

Will and Ramzana started off down the towpath while Brendan dashed in to grab a couple of apples for the ponies, Jupiter and Ginger, who lived on the Meadow. He caught up with them as they reached Polly's boat, *Florian*. It was more compact than *Fair Rosamund* and the prettiest, trimmest canal boat on that stretch of water. Her main bodywork was a rich dark green with details and flourishes picked out in white and red. The outside of the cabin had a painting of a romantic, fairy-tale castle with wisps of white, cloud-like pennants floating from the turrets. On the roof Polly had stationed yellow stencilled growing-boxes with parsley, chives and marjoram for her vegetarian meals.

She was unpinning washing from the line when the trio appeared. Her cheeks were rosy, like the bonny girl on the Ovaltine tin. In keeping with her general life-style, she favoured dungarees, faded cotton prints and thick handknitted jerseys and wore sandals, winter and summer. Polly's real name was the Hon. Paulina Something-Something; and with a legacy to keep her, she pottered about, helping in the health food shop, working with old people and championing worthy causes. Her favourite was a women's group named Sisters All. She and Brendan were great friends and he was a frequent guest, goggling at the telly, drinking hot cocoa and munching popcorn.

George, her elderly golden retriever, thumped his tail on seeing Brendan. Polly, brought up to be as helpful as possible, mused.

'Let's see,' she said trying to be constructive. 'George did bark a couple of times last night, didn't you old boy? But then, that could have been the fox. He's snooping around again. I'll keep my eyes peeled,' she promised.

All the canal boat people were slightly odd in one way or another. Narrow boats were cheaper than houses, but that wasn't the only reason the boat people had decided to live on water rather than on land. They wished to be different. They weren't drop-outs or hippies exactly, more people who liked to be independent. To loosen their moorings and move on somewhere else, if the mood should take them. Brendan always felt people who lived in houses were somehow dull and stodgy compared to them. Living on a boat was one reason he felt different to other children at school. *Lord Nelson*, *Tamar*, *Venice*, *Prudence*, *Queen of Hearts*, *Archmides* made a colourful alternative society to the terraces and semis of Stowbridge. Although, mind you, Stowbridge was not entirely without interest. There was a famous craft museum and an art gallery full of fashionable Victorian paintings which attracted tourists in the season.

Commander Halsey, in his uniform of yachting cap, baggy shorts and guernsey, was touching up the paintwork of the *Lord Nelson*. He had an awful, booming voice and called his wife 'Woman' instead of her name, which was Nell. He always gave Brendan the giggles whenever he opened his mouth. He hadn't seen a greyhound.

Neither had James in the *Tamar*. He always looked as if there was a bad smell very close to him, but today he had obviously been dealing with something of an extremely repellant nature.

'I'll cycle down the towpath and look, after I've finished marking these maths tests . . . this unspeakable charade of miscalculation.' He almost choked as he was speaking. James taught at the Comprehensive and Brendan hoped he wouldn't be in his class when he went there in a couple of years.

Ramzana and Will seemed to have hit it off. Brendan walked behind them, finding it hard not to feel left out and only hearing snatches of their conversation.

'Our houseboats have funny names as well,' Ramzana was saying as they made their way to the Meadow. '*Plum Pudding*, *Rock n' Roll*, *Blue Danube*, *Scherazade*, *Some Enchanted Evening*. . . Ours is called *The Lady of Shalott*.'

Brendan wanted to ask about his father, instead he said, 'Is anyone living in it now?'

'No, it's locked up. If someone doesn't air it soon it'll

start smelling of damp. And there are always repairs, you know.'

'Don't I just,' said Will with a heavy sigh.

They were in the Meadow now, an enormous area of common land which lay between the river and the canal. *The Dog and Duck* pub was the only building on it, about half a mile from where they were.

The sun was beginning to dip down on the far side of the Meadow in that mystical, still time when day meets night and gives way to it. Mallards flew overhead, bottom heavy, beating the air with their wings.

Their cloudy breath rose in the air. Will handed his binoculars to Ramzana.

'See if you can spot Sultan. You know what he looks like.'

Ramzana trained them in every direction but could see nothing that looked like a greyhound. Will took back the binoculars to find their way to the ponies who were grazing close to the river.

A new and wonderful feeling of elation had started to grow in Ramzana. Since his arrival in England, this was the first time he felt free, even slightly light-hearted. His connection with Brendan and his family, the canal boats and being in this wide open space made him feel himself again, the way he used to be in Srinagar. There was always a great expanse of sky at home, reflected in the lake waters. Still or agitated, the waters always contained the sky.

He smelt the damp air and a faint odour of horse manure. The air in the mountains was richer, with pine and woodsmoke, but this was good air too. He sniffed deeply.

Will asked, 'You're not scared of horses, are you?'

They had reached the ponies. Ramzana didn't answer.

He brought his face close to Jupiter and let him nuzzle his ear. He whispered something to the pony and stroked his nose.

'Can I ride him?' he asked.

'He's not saddled. . .'

In a trice Ramzana had sprung on the pony's back and before Will could stop him he had urged Jupiter into a canter, then a gallop and a second later they were flying across the Meadow. 'Hoash, hoash,' they heard him call. Brendan and Will stood gaping as the pony and Ramzana, riding barebacked and bridleless, became smaller and smaller in the distance. They reappeared, a few minutes later, both panting and breathless. Ramzana, flushed with excitement, leaped off and gave the pony a farewell pat.

'Where on earth did you learn to ride like that?' demanded Will. He didn't sound cross, just admiring. 'You should be in a circus!'

'In Kashmir, on my cousin's ponies. He has four and he takes tourists up to the glacier beyond Gulmarg.'

Brendan felt a little jealous. What a performer! He wished he could ride. He wished now that he had taken up Will's offer to give him riding lessons last autumn. It would have been fun going with Ramzana. He looked at him with growing respect.

It was cold. Will pulled his Afghan jacket closer.

'May as well call in at the *Dog and Duck*.'

Brendan was appalled. 'You don't think he'd tell us anything?' He was walking next to Ramzana and he took his anorak sleeve. 'You know Simon Thripp in 4S? The one who's always bragging and showing off – Tariq's best friend? He lives over there in that pub. His dad's Frank Thripp, the landlord. Well, *he's* been trying to get this path,' (a rough

23

country track, pitted and puddled) 'changed to a tarred road.'

Brendan stopped, all worked up, so Ramzana had to stop as well. 'You know why?' he asked rhetorically. 'So cars can come up this path. And he can make lots of money. Simon's told everyone that they're going to sell up when they've made millions and millions and go and live in Portugal, in a villa, with a swimming pool and a maid.'

'That's it,' said Will. 'Exploit nature, make money, spend it on TVs and microwaves and villas and don't give a damn about the environment.'

Brendan looked at him crossly. Couldn't he ever lay off his bugbear? Ignoring Will, he went on, 'Those tourists we get in the summer. Well, Frank Thripp wants coach-loads of them in his pub.'

It was lighting-up time. Stars were pricking the indigo sky like tips of the finest embroidery needles. Even though it was a mile away, the lights of the railway station painted long, yellow reflections in the puddles of rainwater. A train rattled by with a warning hoot of two mournful notes, starting high and falling low singing 'down we go'.

The *Dog and Duck* looked a cosy haven, with white-washed walls and thatched roof. The boys watched through the window as Will went in to ask after Sultan. Frank Thripp was polishing glasses and only gave him a brief look. He shook his head and turned to more important matters, like wiping the bar counter.

'Even if he had seen Sultan, he'd rather choke than tell me,' Will laughed as they walked back to the canal.

'Sorry we didn't hear anything, Ramzana. What about a notice in Mr Khan's shop?' He scratched his head, tilting his cap almost over his eyes.

No list of genius ideas for once, thought Brendan.

Will was anxious to wind up the evening. 'Well, it was really nice getting to know you.' He shook Ramzana's hand. 'Come over and see us again, won't you? And keep in touch about the dog.' Brendan could tell that he'd really taken a shine to him.

Ramzana turned right at the towpath and they turned left to go home and make arrangements for the emergency meeting of the SCOM committee.

3

The sky over the Meadow was different each day, each hour even. In the pale blue haze of summer it could be as remote and abstract as an idea. Or, when heavy grey clouds sagged over it, a vortex. And the light – Brendan shaded his eyes against the pure oyster-coloured light of the Spring afternoon.

He was standing on the edge of its great expanse. In front of him, three miles away, Hunter's Wood dipped gently down to the basin of the Meadow. A sparrow-hawk hung in the air a little way off. He wondered on what it had set its sights. Probably a song-thrush.

Here his mind seemed to empty of its usual matter, the space and the light and the air conjuring other thoughts and speculations. One of his favourite imaginings was the heart of the Meadow going thump, thump, thump. He liked to imagine its support reaching the complex, secret life underneath its surface. If only he could hear the activity of the growing spring vegetation! The heavings and the pushings and the minute unfurlings of campion, daisy, violet and catchfly. The queen wasps chewing woodpulp for their nests, woodlice, ground beetles and every kind of minibeast scurrying in the dense roots of couch grass and sheep's fescue. Spiders floating in the wind, spinning links and turning double somersaults.

Hummings and rustlings, tremblings, throbbings and minute-sounding poppings. Soon crickets would start stridulating. He smiled as he thought of last summer when he had caught a whole jar of them in a field and released them in his own Meadow. He loved the sound of their chirruping when they touched wings and legs together.

He began walking towards the west, his wellies squelching in the boggy ground, still saturated from winter rain. From a distance, the puddles appeared as blind as windowpanes. A great herd of geese honked incessantly by the river. Last summer had been unusually hot and dry, with temperatures in the eighties. One evening at sunset, walking in exactly this direction, he had seen burning flames appear in the hoof marks and potholes in the ground. It had been quite uncanny. Some very special refraction of the light of the setting sun.

Jupiter and Ginger saw him approach and whinnied softly. He had a currycomb with which to groom them and two apples for a Sunday treat. As he worked on the ponies, he thought of the evening before and Ramzana's dare-devil ride. He'd never before experienced anything like it; almost as if he'd seen Ramzana's real self, his soul. He clenched his teeth involuntarily. It was time to get back to the boat and the scom meeting. Time to get involved.

Like most scom meetings, the latest emergency meeting was a cross between business and a rather riotous social occasion. All the canal boat dwellers and a few others were jammed into the cabin of *Fair Rosamund*, and were getting high on Thornbridge Best Bitter and impassioned talk. No wonder, thought Brendan, they weren't taken seriously.

Will clapped his hands in an effort to introduce some order. No one paid any attention. 'Scandalously corrupt councillors . . . running our affairs like their own private enterprise . . . how much do you think Thripp gave them? . . . looks like we're done for now . . . last date for the Appeal is early next month . . . I'm thoroughly disillusioned with the Nature Council . . . ' Everyone was intent on airing their views.

'Ladies and gentlemen,' Will was shouting. 'Order, order . . . What we need now is a firm plan of action. Petitions and letters to the paper haven't worked . . . '

'That's right,' boomed the voice of Commander Halsey. 'Something short and sharp. That's what's needed. Make them sit up.'

'Suggestions please . . . '

Brendan listened glumly, trying to control an over-whelming urge to knock a couple of the committee's heads together. One definitely Will's. He tried to work out who the other most deserving candidate could be. Yak, yak, yak. That's all the SCOM campaign had ever amounted to. Anyone with sense could see it would take more than polite protests to stop the road from going ahead. Action, that's what was needed. He thumped his fist on the floor. Direct and dramatic action.

Polly dug him in the ribs.

'Don't look so cross,' she whispered. 'Want to come over for a goggle tomorrow?'

Brendan was in no mood to be humoured. He wound his fingers round his hair. What could he, personally, do. What could be done to prevent Frank Thripp from getting his way?

'All right, so we go to Appeal.' Will's voice rose above the babel. 'Then suppose the Appeal fails. Do we go on after that? It'll mean legal proceedings in the High

Court and that means a barrister. That'll cost us a few thousand. Can we take it on? Not an easy proposition. Let's have a show of hands. Those in favour of going the whole hog?'

There was an overwhelming response. Only James held back and when he saw how far he was outnumbered, he muttered, 'Oh, well, I suppose I'll have to go along as well.'

In the end a grand plan was drawn up. Clara scribbled down notes. First of all an Action Day, with a march and a meeting in the Town Hall. Then presentation of the Appeal. If all failed they would look for a barrister to take the case to the High Court. The finances could be dealt with later.

Naturally, thought Brendan wryly, money grew on trees.

It was late by the time everyone left. Brendan didn't wait for the post-mortem but took himself off to his cabin to try and think. He sat for a long time, literally feeling himself racking his brains, but no brilliant solution presented itself. Rupert Bear would have come up with an answer: get the Chinese Princess to put a spell on the *Dog and Duck*, or kidnap Simon Thripp and hold him to ransom until his dad withdrew his planning application.

He sniffed impatiently. He had to stop fantasizing and think *clearly*. Suddenly, he thought of Ramzana. He seemed reliable and, well, calm. Not like those hot-air experts in the boat tonight. He'd talk it over with him and see if he wanted to join him. But, whatever they decided, they would keep it to themselves. No grown-ups, no Will or Clara, just the two of them.

'Well, what did you think?' Will asked at supper the next night. 'I thought we covered a lot, don't you?'

He was in one of his chummy moods.

Brendan said cuttingly, 'You all just go on and on. Everyone's got to have their say. It's so . . . so . . . *inefficient*. It takes for ever and then it doesn't work out.'

'What do you suggest we do then?' Will asked evenly.

Clara, who was starting to wash up, laughed. 'We're only trying to be democratic.'

'What's that mean?' Brendan asked.

'You know, a fair hearing for everyone. Each person's opinion to be taken into account. It's from the Greek, *demos*, people.'

'I bet Frank Thripp doesn't have a committee to work things out with. He just does what he feels like.'

'That's right. He's a one man tyrant. A dictator, if you like.' Will sounded as though he was in agreement with Brendan. 'But,' he said, putting his mug down with a flourish, 'also remember that dictatorships don't last long.'

'Thought you liked dictators, like that Stalin. Thought you were a Marxist.'

'Socialist, actually,' Will said loftily. 'I don't believe in the *private* accumulation of wealth. I could go on for hours about my political beliefs, but I've got a lot of filing to do.' He started drying up.

'Look Bren, have you got a brilliant idea you're sitting on? I mean, how do *you* think we ought to go about it? What would you do?'

'I'd go straight to Downing Street and see the Prime Minister. It's a matter of national importance.'

'Well, you're free to try,' Will grinned infuriatingly. 'We won't stop you.'

The most important things in Brendan's life were Clara, the boat and the Meadow. The Meadow was as much a part of his domestic landscape as if it had been his own back yard. That's what made life on the boat so different. Being so cramped, you couldn't stay inside for long. Once outside its thin shell, he was with the elements and a few steps away was the Meadow. Early in his life he had claimed it for himself. He had imagined it belonged to him and so it did.

When he was little, he surveyed it from his baby-buggy. Clara used to push him out there whenever she got the chance. She had taught him to really look at flowers and snail-shells and at raindrops sliding down blackthorn twigs like cable-cars. She had taught him to paint, to observe detail. First he had absorbed by sight and smell and later discovered the how and why of the Meadow's abundant wildlife. He and Clara had spent hours there together. He knew he would never forget the hot June afternoons, sitting waist-high in buttercups. Paddling in the river with the ducks, surprising larks in the grass so they whirred upwards however quietly he approached them; cobwebs spangled with dew, and hunting for mushrooms in the Autumn. The rabbits, stoats, foxes, weasels, all the birds that came and went, the aquatic life in the ditches, nearly every hole and nest was known to him. On his bedroom shelf sat four slim A4 size exercise books, bound by Clara in marbled covers, full of wonderfully detailed drawings and watercolours, with notes, of what grew and lived in the Meadow. When he thought about a motorable road and the effects of noise and petrol fumes it struck him in the stomach like a pain. Of course it was going to change everything. He felt certain that if he were a beetle or a fieldmouse he'd want to emigrate as far away as possible. Every creature within a quarter of a mile would do the same. Their safe habitat, in which everything was interdependent,

31

and which had slowly evolved to its present state over hundreds of years, would be altered – never to be the same again.

He was careful not to show his books to anyone, least of all at school. He knew what would happen. Teachers loved getting their hands on pupils' 'interests'. He'd be proclaimed the ecology expert and made to do projects on environmental studies. This was his kingdom. No one was going to take it over from him.

He couldn't stand by and allow this precious part of his world to change, especially when the instrument of change was Simon Thripp's dad.

Brendan had been assigned the task of designing the posters for the SCOM Action Day. He was used to doing this job, but now that the committee had decided it was time to raise its collective profile, he was given a title: Publicity Officer.

He sniggered under his breath. It was like calling a rat-catcher an Environmental Health Officer. He ought to have a T-shirt with his grandiose title printed across it.

'What's the silliest slogan you've ever seen on a T-shirt?' he asked Will.

'Can't think. Look, about the publicity. You're responsible for the costing and printing you know. Do a bit of shopping around before you choose your printer.'

Brendan rather enjoyed going to all the local printing shops to get quotes for his posters and flyers. He had designed a stunning screen print of a swan, a horse and a duck cleverly superimposed on one another with Letraset printing that said 'SAVE US. We need your help'. Then he'd put the date, time and venue of the meeting.

Ramzana and Brendan wandered around the school grounds at lunch break, ignoring all the nasty jibes from Simon Thripp and his gang. Ramzana seemed really pleased to be asked to help and immediately offered to put a poster up in the Tandoori.

'We'll go round all the Asian shops,' he said. 'Dada knows them all. And I'll help with the flyers. What about school? They won't mind if we stick one up there.'

The next day Brendan asked if he could display a poster in the staff room and one on the general notice board. He had just finished pinning it up when Simon Thripp came down the corridor. As soon as he'd read what it said, he gave Brendan a violent shove, yanked it off the board and tore it into four pieces. He pushed Brendan against the wall and dug a bony elbow into his ribs.

'So we're having a demo then are we, young Brendan?' he said in a mocking, baby voice.

'Going to save the wee birdies, eh? The duckies and the swansies?' He made a mincing movement.

'Going to pick flowers to press in our folder? Ooh, we're a right little pansy aren't we?'

He punctuated each phrase with a vicious dig in Brendan's ribs. Simon was two years older and reminded Brendan of a fox, with his poll of orange-coloured hair and his narrow, mean looking face. Except foxes were far more interesting than Simon Thripp. He looked at Brendan contemptuously through narrowed, pale green eyes.

His lieutenant, Tariq Haider, a bustling bully of a boy, with a puffed-up chest like a pigeon, giggled weakly like a wobbly spring and leaned against the board in a studiedly nonchalant pose.

'Give it to him, Si!' he shouted.

Other children, drawn by the smell of battle began to gather and Ramzana came running in from the playground. He went up to Tariq and stuck his face in front of his.

'You *ulloo*,' he swore. Tariq's chest puffed up even more.

'Call me an *ulloo*,' he yelled in outrage. 'Who do you think you are?' He fired off lots of nasty-sounding abuse in Urdu and began to pummel Ramzana, who easily dodged him.

'Kashmiri dog! Dirty Anglo-Indian! Why don't you go back to Kashmir and let the Indian soldiers put you in jail like your father?'

Shocked by what he had heard, Brendan jerked his head and caught Simon's chin with a satisfying crack. He felt his grip loosen and turned on him energetically.

The onlookers cheered. Much to their disappointment, the commotion only lasted a few moments before the staff room door flew open and Mr Bulmer appeared looking furious. He advanced menacingly towards the group.

'I heard some very unpleasant things being said. You wouldn't by any chance be wanting to go to the Head's office now, would you? What's going on? I want an explanation.'

'He called me a poof,' said Brendan, pointing at Simon.

'You will apologize this instant,' said Mr Bulmer magisterially.

Brendan was hotly indignant. 'He called me that because I'm a conservationist. And he tore up my poster,' he scuffed the torn-up pieces on the floor. His ribs hurt where Simon had been digging into them. He hoped Mr Bulmer would give him the telling-off he deserved.

Mr Bulmer raised one eyebrow, a much copied mannerism in his class.

'A conservationist, hmm? Do you by any chance refer to your campaign against the tarred road on the Meadow? Does that qualify you as a conservationist?'

Brendan remembered that part of the problem of getting enough support for the SCOM campaign was that not everyone agreed about the threat of a road. Lots of people were sympathetic to Frank Thripp's business enterprise. There had been comments about un-neighbourly feelings and storms in tea-cups. Mr Bulmer looked at him reflectively.

'Grand words, Brendan. Grand words.'

Brendan regretted his outburst. He wished the whole incident would blow over quickly. No good saying too much. Mr Bulmer might suddenly take it into his head to get him to write about wildflowers on the Meadow, or classify birds on the canal for a maths project.

The poster in the staff room stayed up, but the Head decided it wasn't suitable for the general noticeboard. Simon Thripp gave Brendan murderous looks every time he saw him. He and Tariq swaggered round school with carefully squared shoulders telling everyone it wouldn't be in their interests to speak to either Brendan or Ramzana.

Brendan didn't care. He'd never belonged to any gang, nor did he like feeling part of a crowd, and Ramzana was too new to have any established friendships. Yet their friendship grew after this. They each had proved their loyalty to one another.

Friday evenings were Brendan's best time of the week, but Friday mornings were the pits. He never hated school as much as he did when he had to go with a group of other children for 'reading help' and handwriting.

Mr Bulmer had raised the matter with Clara and Will

at the start of the year, but to his immense relief neither had seemed particularly bothered. Normally, when he informed parents that their little darlings were behind in reading and just about borderline educationally subnormal, they would launch into lengthy diatribes about the last year's teacher, or look threateningly at Mr Bulmer.

Mr Bulmer disliked parents' meetings and always tried to placate parents of slow children with some cheery remarks about how good they were at clearing up and giving out rulers and pencils.

'He's got an astonishing grasp of environmental science. Knows just about everything to do with birds and plants.' Then he quickly slipped in, 'But he's at the level of an eight-year-old as far as his reading goes.'

'Oh I never worry about Brendan,' his mother was airily reassuring. 'He knows all sorts of things we don't. He'll probably end up being a gardener or a forester. I shouldn't worry too much about him,' and she smiled disarmingly.

But Mr Bulmer's professional conscience had made him arrange for Brendan to be given extra help by a kind old ex-teacher, who gave her services voluntarily to the school.

This Friday morning he was told to look for all the words which contained 'augh' and underline them. Afterwards, Mrs Titchbon had said she would hear him read them. 'Laugh, caught, draught, haughty.' He went about his task with his mind on the afternoon deliciously looming ahead.

Ramzana was coming to tea. They could mess around the canal, go fishing; there was the swan's nest about a mile up-stream that he was keeping an eye on. They would take the dinghy and a picnic.

Mrs Titchbon interrupted his thoughts by settling herself next to him to check his work.

'I've joined SCOM,' she confided, showing her large yellow teeth. 'They said I'd be working under you in Publicity. I've been asked to do the press releases, but I think the posters and flyers are more important.'

Brendan thought she was trying too hard. He felt a twinge of resentment. Why should he have to work with a teacher from school? But then he remembered that the real campaign wasn't going to involve any grown-up. Once he and Ramzana had thought about what to do, they would just get on with it. He nodded briefly and bent over his work again. Mrs Titchbon must have got the message that Brendan wasn't all that enthusiastic about their new partnership and she soon got up and didn't refer to it again.

4

The way home was along a dreary brick wall down Carswell Street on which someone had graffitied, 'What happened to the dinosaur?' Then you turned left at the High Street, through a smelly little alley next to a pub, known as The Cut, right into Gribble Road, then Nixey's Lane with Tom Wilson's builder's yard on one side and straight on to the canal and *Fair Rosamund*.

Sometimes, Brendan amused himself by timing his journey home. By pretending to be someone else, he would try to imagine how long it might take to get to the boat. Twice as long for a woman in high heels compared to Gary Lineker; with an incontinent dog that insisted on every lamp-post, twenty minutes. Eight for a skate-boarder and so on. Today he decided to be a drunkard, with one leg shorter than the other.

He set off with his right leg on the pavement and his left in the gutter, so he would be facing the oncoming traffic. Unfortunately the experiment was shortlived. A large lady cyclist swung into Carswell Road from the High Street and nearly crashed into him as he teetered along in what he imagined to be a state of intoxication. She was one of those serious bikers wearing the full regalia of skin-tight black shorts, helmet and reflective strips, her machine sporting bulging panniers from every conceivable bar on her machine. Sweating and red-faced, she managed to avoid him by swerving dangerously.

'Stupid git!' she shouted.

Brendan grinned and ran the rest of the way home. Ramzana had got there before him and was chatting to Clara.

'I'm so glad about Sultan,' she was saying.

A farmer had found the dog skulking about near his outhouses and had telephoned the Animal Sanctuary. Apart from looking more starved than usual, Sultan was fine.

'Bashir Chacha wants to come and thank you for searching for him.'

'Any time Ramzana. Tell him he's welcome to drop in for a cup of tea. Look boys, I've got to dash now with this order, but get yourselves a drink and something to eat. I won't be long.' Clara packed her finished picture carefully into her rucksack and pedalled away on her bike.

'Can I look round your boat?'

'Let's go for a row.'

Both boys spoke simultaneously. There was an easy-going feeling between them that had developed in the short time they had become friends, cemented by the fight with Simon and Tariq. Ramzana was longing to compare the narrowboat with his houseboat. There were familiar things about this territory but he wanted to make sure, almost find his bearings again.

He had lost his mother, his father and his home all in the space of a few months. Sometimes he felt like a blind person, just managing to keep on course with Dada and Bashir's help. Now he felt ready to find his own way.

'Do you ever move your boat? I mean do you travel to other places on the canal?'

'No, we haven't got an engine and this is a fixed mooring, so we pay rent and everything,' replied Brendan. He led the way to the stern end. He couldn't hold in his curiosity about Ramzana's father. 'What was that Tariq said about your dad? Is he really in jail?' the words just came out.

'Yeah. Somewhere in Kashmir.'

'But why? What did he do?'

'Nothing really. There's a sort of war going on. He's a political prisoner. You see Kashmir's a part of India, but some Kashmiris want to go over to Pakistan, some want to stay with India and he's caught in the middle. The Indian Army thought he was helping terrorists and smuggling in Kalashnikovs and bombs from Pakistan, but it wasn't him. It was our neighbours, but he couldn't say,' and he made a slicing motion with his hand across his throat.

'Haven't you heard from him, then?' Brendan was shocked.

'Not since he was taken away – about four months ago now.'

'That's really tough,' Brendan sympathized.

Ramzana didn't want to go on talking about his father. He looked round the cabin and noted how much living space was squeezed into the forty by six foot space of *Fair Rosamund*. Very much less than *The Lady of Shalott*, which was almost twice as long and wide and which rested high above the water.

The first little room was Clara's exhibition gallery, with all her painted wares. Her tin kettles, dippers and bowls neatly stacked on shelves and hanging from hooks. The bowls sat one on top of the other separated by blue tissue paper to protect the paint. She had decorated the room like an authentic bargee's cabin with cupboards, a fold-away bed and a little black cast-iron stove. The surfaces were treated like a wood grain on which she had painted cabbage shaped roses in pinks, blues and yellows and the classic fairy-tale castle, the two motifs common to all traditional narrowboats. The walls were hung with china plates with faggotted edges through which lace and ribbon were threaded.

Ramzana was impressed. 'It's like a museum,' he exclaimed.

Brendan stood on the top step which led to the stern deck and the big 'ram's head' tiller.

'This is where the boatmen steered from. They kept their feet warm, but they could still see over the cabin roof.' Even the panels on the hatches were painted with roses.

Will and Clara had the next room. There was a double bed draped with festoons of flowered chintz, swagged and arranged to look like the curtains on a four-poster. Between this and Brendan's room was the bathroom which had a proper bath, a basin and a chemical loo. Brendan's room had a bunk bed, a cupboard in the wall, some shelves and a small chair and desk space. Every inch of wall space, including the cupboard door, was covered with sketches and watercolours.

'These are really good,' Ramzana said, admiring them.

'Oh, they're nothing. I did them ages ago. My mum's the artist in the family.'

Outside the window, Ramzana could see poplars on the opposite bank. A massive bramble bush tangled on the nearside and the bank was almost level with his chin. Reflections from the canal made changing, watery patterns on the ceiling. It was possible to believe there was no ordinary connection with the world going about

41

its business outside. Just like the houseboat, thought Ramzana contentedly.

Brendan took down his exercise books from the shelf and opened one to show Ramzana. He leafed through it slowly.

'You're brilliant. You *are* an artist. Have you shown these to Mr Bulmer?'

'No.' Brendan was alarmed but pleased at his reaction. 'And you're not to say anything at school. Do you promise?' Ramzana nodded.

Brendan jabbed the notebooks with a finger. 'If the road happens, all this is going to be affected'. He told Ramzana at some length about his disgust with the way SCOM was conducting the campaign. He looked at him for a sign of solidarity.

'I'm thinking of going to London to see the Prime Minister. Do you want to come?'

Ramzana pondered the situation. 'It's a bit early, isn't it? I mean, why don't we wait until the Action Day and the Appeal's over and see what happens. If nothing works, then we could think about it.' He sounded impartial and reasonable.

Brendan didn't meet his eye for some minutes. Ramzana could see that his answer had disappointed, even angered, him. Brendan pushed his hair out of his eyes and stood up. A notebook fell on the floor and he made no attempt to pick it up. Ramzana handed it to him.

'I suppose so,' he said sulkily.

He set about busying himself in the galley making jam sandwiches, cutting cake and getting some squash.

His mood slowly improved once they were on the water, rowing the dinghy in the direction of the swan's nest. He pointed out water rats' lairs and a hole where he had once seen an adder as they travelled upstream past the pretty narrow gardens of canalside cottages. The swan was sitting humped on her nest, so Brendan knew the eggs were still there. Last spring someone had got to the nest and smashed them. They had their tea and started back.

Ramzana took the oars, setting off with the easy, graceful swing of a born sculler. They were fairly racing downstream when suddenly a large motor-boat which had been idling on the banks began a full-scale throttle towards them.

'Look out!' Brendan could see the powerful boat advancing dangerously close but Ramzana's back was to it. He glanced over his shoulder and with practised skill, stalled his left oar and swung their little tub over to the bank, out of harm's reach. He didn't seem alarmed.

'We've got two little shikaras that belong to our houseboat. One's mine and one was my mother's. We used to go for picnics and get my mother's shopping in them. It was great going over the side for a swim.' He stroked strongly. 'There are miles and miles of lotus beds in the lake,' he continued, eager to tell Brendan more about his life back home. 'I used to pick the lotus flowers and sell them to tourists for lots of money,' he laughed, his eyes full of merriment at the joke, which was that the tourists could have picked them for nothing themselves.

The dinghy tied up, they went inside the boat. Brendan lit a couple of lamps and emptied the bilges, which was his job. The lamps were done by whoever happened to be around at dusk.

'Can I see your drawings again – the ones in the books?' asked Ramzana. Sounds like he's really and truly interested, thought Brendan.

Ramzana pointed out a drawing of a kingfisher, delicately coloured in blues and greens.

'We've got these exact birds in Kashmir.'

He found another bird which also lived in the trees near his houseboat, a green woodpecker. Lots of other birds and plants in Brendan's notebooks seemed to be the same as those at home, although he didn't know their names.

Clara still hadn't come back and Will was away on a kitchen fitting job on the Isle of Wight until the weekend. Footsteps sounded on deck and Polly's bright face looked in through the little doors.

'Hi Brendan. Oh, hello Ramzana. Is Will here? There's someone over at my place who wants to make a booking for the carriage.' She looked pinker in the cheeks than usual and her eyes kept darting to Ramzana.

Brendan gave her Will's whereabouts, and looking distinctly uncomfortable, she said, 'Look, I'll just go over and tell this person what you told me and I might come back if there's a message for Will.' Brendan got the impression that she was keeping something back; it wasn't at all like her. Polly normally blurted out whatever she was thinking about.

Fifteen minutes later she was back.

'Ramzana I need to tell you something,' were the surprising words that emerged as soon as she'd entered the cabin.

She turned to Brendan. 'You've heard of Amnesty International?' He shook his head. She continued. 'It's a very famous organization which tries to check what's happening to people who've been put in jail by their governments – mostly for not agreeing with the government. That's not a crime in most countries.'

Polly raised her eyebrows questioningly to see if the boys had taken in what she was saying.

Ramzana was listening with deep concentration. He asked, 'What if someone's been jailed because there's been a mistake?'

'Exactly. Well, I'm very involved in something just like Amnesty, except it's not as famous. It's called Prisoners Without Trial. We just take on a few local interest cases.' She paused. 'Our executive committee's decided to find out what's happening to Abdul Karim, your dad . . . We want to know if he's in good shape, make sure he's been well treated in jail – you know, getting letters from his family, that sort of thing.'

She looked quite flustered as she made her speech and Ramzana's eyes got bigger and bigger. A few minutes of silence followed.

'You didn't know, did you, that your uncle Bashir approached our organization last month and asked us to help. Someone called Loveleen Tikoo's in *Florian* right now and she's organizing a protest march for your father.' She was out of breath now and blinked nervously. 'She just rang Bashir and asked him if it was all right to tell you about what was going on. I think she wants you to take part in the march.'

'Is a march like those demos on telly?' Brendan demanded. 'Lots of people with banners and flags shouting things like, "No, no, no, we won't let go"?' He raised a clenched fist in the air.

'That's it, Bren.'

Ramzana was almost beside himself with excitement. 'Are they going to use Brendan's dad's carriage and ponies for the march? Is that why she wants to see him?'

Brendan muttered, 'He isn't my dad.'

'Oh, sorry Brendan. I didn't know.' That explained a lot thought Ramzana. Why, for instance, he was so unfriendly towards Will.

'Bren, come *on*. He's your step-dad and he's adopted you,' Polly remonstrated mildly.

Brendan's face took on a mulish expression. Ramzana thought, he's sulking again. But Will's so *nice*.

'Does this Loveleen Tikoo want to see me?' he asked Polly. 'She's got a Kashmiri name, she must be a Kashmiri Brahmin,' he added by way of explanation to the other two. He was on fire with the dramatic news.

'Come on Bren,' he shook his shoulder. You'll have to come with me on this march.'

At least there's one committee that knows how to get things moving, thought Brendan, closing the doors of the boat behind him. He followed Polly and Ramzana, who was doing a kind of dervish dance of delight, whirling and snapping his fingers all the way to the *Florian*.

5

'She looks like a witch,' Brendan pronounced, rattling a stick on the graffitied wall as he and Ramzana walked back to *Fair Rosamund* from school the next day.

'Just like a witch with shiny black hair and that shiny green stuff on her eyes.'

'Full of herself, isn't she? But I bet she gets things done. She looks the kind that does.'

Loveleen Tikoo was tiny, like an exotic china figurine. Sharply dressed in an expensive black suit and teetery high heels she had straight away made a great show of riffling through documents in her formidable looking briefcase. Once she had found the paper she was searching for, she held it up in front of her with exquisitely manicured fingers and read out loud from it.

'This is the provisional plan. We begin the protest march at nine sharp. TV crew and Press get a photo opportunity with Abdul Karim's family. The carriage and marchers proceed down the High Street, along the Shopping Arcade and on to Market Square. The meeting begins at the Buttercross. Speeches, distribution of leaflets, petition to our MP, another photo call, interviews and so on. Meeting over by eleven thirty.'

She wasn't a bit likeable, thought Brendan. But she

had a way of tackling situations which showed that nothing was allowed to stand in her way. She probably didn't waste much time consulting people, he decided. *If* she did, it was to make them feel important. She would push her point of view whatever anyone else said. He remembered his discussion with Will and Clara. Maybe Loveleen Tikoo and Frank Thripp had something in common – a complete belief in themselves. They were the sort who never thought they might be wrong. He summed it up. Selfish but effective.

Ramzana looked rather bemused. He sat silent, eyes wide open, his big ears almost quivering with excitement. All this talk of TV, newspapers, interviews, photo opportunities and speeches was heady stuff. It was obvious that Loveleen was quite at home in that world. So much the better he thought.

'Who's the keynote speaker, Loveleen?' asked Polly.

'S.P. Padgaonker, C.B.E., the famous Human Rights campaigner.' She tossed her sleekly bobbed head. 'We've been very lucky to get him as he's off to Finland next month for the International Human Rights Seminar.'

'Oh, splendid,' Polly enthused. She was clearly much in awe of Loveleen. They made a startling contrast; Polly big and wholesome and flaxen haired, like a milkmaid; Loveleen petite, red-taloned and businesslike.

Loveleen cleared her throat, 'But of course the most important thing as far as the media is concerned is the family. The aged father, the concerned brother and the suffering son.' She fixed Ramzana with her large, heavily made-up eyes.

'We'll have you in national costume, holding a placard. You'll have to look *sad* you know, for the cameras and the Press. You can't underestimate the appeal of a mother and fatherless child.'

48

Brendan thought that was very cheeky, considering she hadn't known Ramzana for more than a quarter of an hour. She continued looking at him as though she was calculating how much pathos could be wrung out of the situation.

Ramzana sensed that she might be using him for her own ends. Her eyes were hard and business-like, even though she was expressing concern for his family. He found, surprisingly, that he didn't really care what she was like as a person as long as she could help him to get something done for his dad. If she was using him, he had no qualms about using her. He found his voice at last. 'When is this going to happen?'

'Saturday, April 26th. That's about a fortnight away isn't it?' She now riffled through a fat Filofax.

'That's our scom Action Day,' Polly said, dismayed.

'I don't know if you'll be able to book Will on that day Loveleen.'

'That is the only possible date,' Loveleen said a little waspishly. 'Our Human Rights celebrity, Mr S.P. Padgaonker, is booked up for months after that.'

The final arrangements would obviously have to wait until Will returned from the Isle of Wight.

'Do try and persuade him', said Loveleen. 'I'll come down and talk to him myself on Sunday if you like. The carriage and ponies will make a big visual impact and that's important for TV.'

'I'll do everything I can,' Polly said soothingly. 'After all, I *am* Vice-chair of scom. Perhaps we can manage to fit in both events.'

'I'm relying on you. Byeeee!' And Loveleen tripped away down the towpath to her waiting car.

'What a mess,' Polly said, rubbing her ear. 'Both

things happening on the same day. It would happen to us, wouldn't it Bren?'

'It's all outside our control,' he proclaimed dramatically, waving his arms to express the scale of the drama. 'But we've got to do something, haven't we?' he challenged Ramzana.

They had nearly reached the boat, when they bumped into Bashir, sauntering along with his dogs. After being introduced to Brendan he said, 'I'm taking these two for a walk, but I thought I might look in and say hello to your mother and father a little later.'

'Stepfather,' murmured Ramzana.

Brendan said he thought Clara would be at home and that he'd tell her. She was making a cake when Bashir knocked on the door half an hour later. She wiped her floury hands and greeted him warmly.

'Come and join us for a cup of tea. These scones are just out of the oven.'

The dogs prostrated themselves gracefully and economically at their master's feet, tongues hanging out and eyes fastened adoringly on him.

Brendan watched as Ramzana's elegantly dressed teenage uncle carefully buttered a scone. His handsome face, with its aquiline nose and dark eyebrows, was set off to perfection by the cut of his navy-blue blazer and cream coloured trousers. He plucked them, to keep the crease, and crossed one leg over the other. An expanse of immaculate white sock descended into highly polished shoes with metal snaffles. His hair was slicked back in a thirties style and he had all the confidence of a glamorous young man-about-town.

His speech was equally elegant and courteous.

'My father and I would like to thank you for all your

trouble.' He glanced at Ramzana. 'You've been terribly kind to my young nephew.' He took another scone.

'We're especially pleased that he's made some friends. It's been lonely for him since he came here.'

Ramzana sat near him. You could tell that the two of them were family, Brendan reflected. Bashir's arm slipped over Ramzana's shoulder and the boy didn't wriggle away. Suddenly, Brendan thought, I wish I had a big brother. Or an uncle. Or a dad.

'Oh, we're so pleased he found us that night,' replied Clara. 'He's welcome to come here any time he wants. Must be a little difficult with you working such long hours. From what I can tell he and Brendan seem to have hit it off.'

Brendan looked quizzically at Ramzana and grinned.

'No, it isn't much fun for him in the restaurant. You see, it doesn't belong to us. The owner, Mr Rana, is a distant cousin from Kashmir. He's a clever businessman all right. The restaurant is only a side-line for him – he's in import-export, money-lending, all kinds of wheeling and dealing. He employs us on slave wages.' He sounded bitter; he obviously wasn't fond of his cousin.

'Can't you work somewhere else?' enquired Clara.

Bashir's handsome face twitched, and he curled his lip.

'My father, bless him, owes Rana quite a lot of money and we're paying it off this way; but interest rates are very high. My father's also got a strange sense of loyalty, something to do with family. And he's got a lot on his mind.'

He looked at Clara. 'You know a little about our problems. My brother's in jail, somewhere in Kashmir, my sister-in-law, Susan, passed away a few months ago. We've got Ramzana to think about. At least we've got a

51

roof over our heads, but that's all it is. Damp, broken furniture, outside loo, the works.'

Clara listened sympathetically, shaking her head in disbelief.

'You should see Rana,' Bashir warmed to his theme. 'Go on, Chhota, describe him.'

Ramzana shifted in his seat. 'Well, he's sort of bulgy and mean looking. And he's very rich.'

'Chhota,' said Bashir plaintively. 'He's a villain. He's *evil*.' He expanded, 'He's a millionaire. He's got a Jaguar XJS with a drinks cabinet and a telephone. Then he's got a brand new BMW *and* a Porsche. He's married to a poor, sweet woman and he has a Chinese girl friend called Lily.'

He took a last swallow of tea.

'However, I've got plans. I'll come and tell you about them one day Mrs Dangerfield, if I may. But right now, I've got to get back to the old chop-house.'

Carswell Road Middle School was quite ordinary in all respects. It didn't have a brilliant Art Department, nor did pupils ever win prizes in poetry-writing competitions. Once a fourth year had fallen into a river trying to rescue her dog and the paper had carried a picture of her with the caption, 'HEROINE KYLIE RESCUES HER PET'. However, it did have a certain reputation for its cricket. Mr Bulmer, when the mood took him, gave the keen cricketers coaching. He was a deck-chair enthusiast and liked to demonstrate his batting and bowling techniques on the school playground.

Although they were only an eight-a-side team, the Eastern Rovers as they called themselves, led by Simon and Tariq did manage to win the occasional match. Simon's bowling was wildly inaccurate, but he had a

30 yard run-in, flailed his arms like windmills and struck terror in the breasts of rival teams. An important match against Larkmead School was coming up and he and Tariq were holding 'trials' for more home talent.

Ramzana badly wanted to join the team and the coaching sessions with Mr Bulmer.

'You'll never get taken,' Brendan warned him. 'They're terrible snobs, and anyway we're at war with them.'

Nonetheless he went ahead for the trials and was told to go through his paces to display his bowling skills. Immediately after, Tariq and Simon went into a huddle to consult and then called him over to say, predictably, that there was no place for a slow bowler that season. Ramzana couldn't hide his disappointment.

'Idiots!' shouted Brendan. Ramzana had a beautiful action and a lingering, accurate googly throw. 'Snobs! Korean Bow-wows!'

'Shut up Dangerfield. We're going to *get* you,' Tariq retaliated.

'One day,' Ramzana stuck his hands in his pockets, 'when we've got enough people I'll teach you to play a game called *Pitoo*. It's nearly as much fun as cricket.'

The bell went for class. 'Are you coming back this afternoon?' Brendan asked him. 'I'm going to start that magpie tally I was telling you about. I've seen a lot of broken eggs near the trees on the Meadow. I'm sure it's magpies. It'll be interesting to find out how many thieves there are.'

'Don't forget we've still got to take round the rest of the flyers. Better do them before Will comes back.'

Will had been away the best part of the week, and Brendan, much to his surprise, found that he didn't mind too much about his imminent return the next day.

6

Will was pleased to be back home again.

'Phew, such hard work. We were working most nights,' he said, settling his silly hat on the back of his head. 'Amazing place, though. A Victorian mansion being done up for an American millionaire. Crenallated battlements, stained glass windows, suits of armour all over the place.'

He made himself comfortable for the evening, with a bottle of his favourite beer.

'Well, what's the news? Fill me in.'

Clara told him about Bashir's visit and Brendan described their encounter with Loveleen Tikoo.

'Can you take on her booking, as well as chair the meeting at the Town Hall?' Clara asked.

'Shouldn't be impossible. She only wants me until eleven-thirty and we start at the Town Hall at twelve. It'll be a tight squeeze. Anyway, it's for poor old Ramzana's father, and you know I've got a soft spot for Yuman Tights.'

Any lingering doubts were efficiently banished by a hefty dose of charm from Ms Tikoo. She came the next day, driving her smart little silver-grey Volkswagen Golf to the very edge of the canal by *Fair Rosamund*.

'Oh Mr Dangerfield . . . ' she cooed.

'Will,' corrected Will.

'I've heard so much about you. I believe you're the only person in the county who can do this for us. If you could *possibly* fit us in, I'll offer you 25 per cent over your standard rates.' She batted her eyes and lit up a cigarette, to Clara's annoyance.

'Do say yes, Will,' she pleaded.

'She's a go-getter all right. Did you see how she went goo-goo with her eyes at Will?' Clara said to Brendan afterwards.

The next two weeks were hectic. Impromptu meetings on the boat most nights as committee members dropped in to draft and re-draft a suitable text for the Appeal. There were more flyers and posters to be printed and distributed. Ramzana suggested taking one to the Asian Cultural Forum on the other side of town and Brendan was surprised at the somewhat chilly reception they were given.

The Secretary of the Forum had some difficulty in realizing that the scom campaign was a different issue to the protest march for Ramzana's father.

'It's the same day,' he said suspiciously.

He agreed to put up their poster only after he had spoken to Clara on the telephone.

'A lot of the Asians don't want to get mixed up with my family because it's a political issue,' Ramzana explained. 'You see, they think we're sitting on the fence. Either we ought to be pro-Pakistan or pro-India and we're neither. We're just Kashmiri.'

'Sounds a bit like Northern Ireland,' Brendan remarked. He had a vague awareness of the troubles in that part of the world.

On Friday, Clara who'd been running round all day opted out of preparing the evening meal.

'I'm exhausted,' she said collapsing in her chair. 'It's bread and cheese tonight boys.'

'Let's get a take-away from the Kashmiri Tandoori,' suggested Will.

'Brendan, you wouldn't mind fetching it, would you? What about bhoona scampi, rice, chicken tikka and peas and potato curry?' He wrote down the order on the back of an envelope.

Brendan trudged off down the towpath towards Bow Bridge. It was only ten minutes away. The evenings were getting longer and the trees were fatly in bud, leaves ready to uncurl like babies' fists. Birds sang in the hedgerows and a lone fisherman peacefully smoked his pipe.

This was his first visit to the Kashmiri Tandoori. He wondered what it was like inside and whether he would meet Ramzana's grandfather.

The restaurant didn't open until seven and there was a CLOSED sign askew on the other side of the smoked glass door. No one seemed to be around; there was no bell or knocker, so he rattled the letter-flap. There was no response from within, so he shouted, 'Ramzana!'

A sash window flew up on the first floor and Bashir looked down. He was wearing a white singlet and mowing his face with a battery-operated razor.

'Coming!' he shouted back cheerily. He opened the door and Brendan went in. Spluttering noises and the clashing of pots and pans came through the door leading to the kitchen. From upstairs the cacophony of a full-scale disco funnelled down the stairwell.

'Come up while I finish dressing.' Bashir bounded upstairs again. Brendan tried to make out the words of the song.

Oh Caroline, oh Caroline,
You're so la-azy, you're so cr-aazy,
You're so attractive,
Oh Ca-ro-line.

He found the sentiments a little baffling. There was a
poster of James Dean in a moody pose by the utilitarian
mirror in which Bashir was slicking back his hair.

'Not exactly swish, is it?'

Brendan didn't volunteer an opinion. He looked at
the bare floorboards. A more dismal habitation would
have been hard to find.

Bashir winked at him in the mirror. 'I *hate* it, I
loathe it. Wish I could stamp on it. Ramzana's gone
to buy some coffee. We've run out. He'll be back any
second.'

The phone rang downstairs.

'Excuse me . . . must get it before the old man. Come
down,' he yelled as he raced downstairs.

Brendan followed him and sat down at a table while
Bashir took his call. He spoke softly with his hand cupped
over the receiver, nervously looking over his shoulder
from time to time.

Meanwhile Brendan was quite content to look around
the restaurant. The walls were covered with dark-red
flocked paper, like cut-velvet; the tables ranged against
the walls, each in its little alcove under a plaster arch.
They were laid with pink, starched linen and dressed
with tiny vases of carnations and fern. Next to the kitchen
door was the bar, an elaborate affair of bamboo and mir-
rors which reflected myriads of bottles of drink. A string
of coloured light bulbs gave it a festive air. What would
diners think if they wandered upstairs? There couldn't
have been a greater contrast, Brendan mused, between

57

the luxury downstairs and the starkness in Ramzana's room.

Bashir finished his call and sat next to Brendan.

'Sorry, that was my girlfriend, Djamila. Father doesn't know we're going steady . . . or, at least, I don't think he does.' He reflected for a moment. 'In fact I may as well tell you, Djamila and I are engaged. We'll be getting married in a few months.' He lowered his voice for effect. 'But don't let on to Father about us, will you? By the way, I'd like your mum to meet Djamila. Shall I bring her over soon?'

Brendan said he was sure it would be all right.

'Where are Tipoo and Sultan?'

'In the back yard. I'll take them for a walk after we've closed. I usually meet Djamila at Bow Bridge at half-past eleven if it's not raining.'

'I've come for a take-away. They said could you go easy on the hot stuff?' Brendan read out the list.

'No problem. And this is on the house, O.K.? Come and meet Father and the crew.'

He led the way. Through the glare of neon lights and the haze of frying oil, Brendan saw Ghulam Ali. Strong, unmatched smells of garlic, ginger, onions and spices filled the atmosphere. Ghulam Ali knocked some sauce off a ladle with a couple of firm taps, balanced it across a pan and turned to meet Brendan. He wiped his hands on his apron and with a big smile on his face pumped his hand for at least a minute.

He was short, only a little taller than the eleven-year-old boy. He had a magnificent white beard with traces of red henna-dye in it. His eyes were soft and brown and he wore a lacy skull-cap on his head.

'You are a very good boy.' His voice was full of approval. 'You make friends with Ramzana. I like you.

I like your family. Ramzana very sad; his mummy gone,'
he pointed upwards, 'his papa locked up. Ramzana
very happy be your friend. Allah will bless you and
keep you.' He patted Brendan's shoulder affection-
ately.

The two helpers were called over and given a rapid
run through of Brendan's identity, whereupon they too
shook his hand and smiled warmly.

'Now,' said Ramzana's grandfather. 'Your Mummy-
Daddy wanting curry? I make first-class curry for them.
Soon ready. You go sit, have coca-cola, ice-cream, any-
thing you like. Bashir!' It was an order.

In ten minutes the food was ready and tied up in
a neat parcel. He wouldn't let Brendan give him any
money. Brendan was embarrassed. He offered Bashir
the £10 note which Will had given him.

'No, no,' Ghulam Ali waved it away fiercely. 'Tell
Mummy-Daddy I come to see them. I want to meet
respected parents. Very nice boy,' he repeated.

Just as Brendan was leaving, Ramzana appeared
with the coffee and a newspaper under his arm.

'Bed-time reading,' he grinned. 'See you tomorrow?'

Ramzana came soon after they had eaten lunch. His
newspaper was folded up under his arm.

'What have you got there?' enquired Brendan.

'Oh, just a paper. I read them when I've got nothing
better to do,' he replied casually. He said to Clara, 'My
grandfather's coming to see you soon and Bashir wants
to bring Djamila over tomorrow.'

'I hope they don't all arrive at the same time,' Clara
laughed. 'I mean for Bashir's sake. Ramzana, that was a
really delicious meal last night. I've just written a thank
you note to Bashir and your grandfather. Will you give

it to them and say I'm looking forward to seeing them.' She gave him a card in an envelope.

Ramzana motioned to Brendan to come away and they went out on the deck.

'I want to show you something, but not here. Let's go to the Meadow.'

Once they were on the way to the Meadow, out of Clara's hearing, Brendan asked, 'What's the secret, then?'

Ramzana unfolded his newspaper, turned back the pages to make it easier to read in the breeze and pointed to a picture of a girl holding something in her hands, like an award.

Ramzana read: 'Concerned Conservationist. Nyree Dawn Dipper has been awarded the Young Country-person's Award of the Year for her successful campaign against a local pond being developed into a marina. Nyree (12) who lives in Little Grinling, Wilts., led a determined campaign against developers. She collected over 3,000 signatures for a petition, wrote articles for her local paper, appeared on radio and television to talk about the effect of development on wildlife and the environment. "I'm simply thrilled that the pond will stay the way it is," she said to reporters.'

He creased the paper into neat folds again. 'Well, what do you think?'

'It's absolutely brill.' Brendan pushed his hair back excitedly. 'We've got to get hold of this girl and ask her how she began and how long it took her. Come on, let's find out where she lives and contact her.' He was impatient to start at once.

'Hold on, hold on,' Ramzana said in his calm voice. 'There's only a week to go until next Saturday's meeting.

Then the Appeal's going to take at least three weeks. There's no hurry.'

'You're wrong. There isn't any time to lose. We must get on with it *now*.'

The very things he liked about Ramzana, his calmness and sensible way of going about things, were getting on Brendan's nerves. However, as it turned out the week got busier and busier, what with school and errands and preparations for Saturday. They managed to find out Nyree's address and telephone number through directory enquiries, but the 'follow through' would have to wait.

7

'She wants the carriage and ponies dolled up like a Christmas tree; buntings and tinsel, and I think she even said fresh flowers.'

'I hope Madam Loveleen doesn't think it's included in the estimate. Quite a prima donna, isn't she? All over the papers this week,' Clara said with barely disguised hostility.

Will chuckled, 'I hear she's got political ambitions. Wants to run for the Council.'

What with the steady stream of visitors and the phone going all the time, there had been no time for housework. The living room cabin was littered with papers and files and mugs with the dregs of old coffee and tea. Clara had decided it was time for a blitz since Bashir and Djamila were dropping in later in the afternoon. She hadn't had the heart to tell them not to come that week, but secretly hoped the phone would ring saying they couldn't make it.

They did come, with the dogs, just as Brendan was taking an enormous black polythene bag of rubbish to the dump. By the time he returned Bashir was tackling a large plate of assorted biscuits. Clara apologized to Djamila. 'Sorry, there's been no time to bake anything. We're up to here,' she said, holding her palm level with her eyebrows.

Brendan took in the scene thinking that although Bashir was glamorous enough on his own, he and Djamila together could have stepped out of a fashion magazine. They were a knockout.

Djamila wore a tiny black skirt which showed almost the whole length of her very long legs, lots of silver jewellery, and kept tossing back her mane of curly black hair. Brendan was awed into silence by this vision of self-confident stylishness. He couldn't help thinking his mother looked positively washed out by comparison. Djamila's style included strong opinions; she was clever too – three A-Levels at the County High.

'Of course my family know we're engaged, but we haven't told them we're getting married this summer. Dad and Mum like Bashir a lot, but his father's going to have a fit when he finds out.'

'Bit of a problem with religion,' added Bashir. 'You see our family's Sunni and hers is Shia. We're both Muslims, but it's worse than being Catholic and Protestant. Her parents don't mind, but it's my dad again. So we thought the best thing was to get married and sort everything out afterwards.'

'That won't be easy,' said Brendan trying to say something appropriate. He helped himself to a chocolate biscuit. He didn't want Djamila to think that he was too young to sympathize with their situation.

'No more studying then?' Will asked handing Djamila a cup of tea.

She made a face. 'I'm sick of studying. Bashir and I are going to run our own restaurant.' She glanced at Clara. 'Hasn't he told you? The first floating tandoori in Britain.'

'Sounds like a great idea,' said Will. 'How are you going to finance it? Bank loan?'

'Her dad's Mr Tasty Kebab,' Bashir said with pride in his voice. 'He's got a chain of fast food restaurants in three counties and he's promised to buy a boat and set us up.'

'Hey Brendan, what about you and Ramzana joining us as washer-uppers?'

Brendan made a face, although he was quite flattered at being included in their plans.

'We're having a fight about the name of the restaurant. Can you help us decide?' Djamila asked Clara. '*I* want to call it *Stella Asiatica*, but this old stick-in-the-mud says no one will get it.'

'*Star of Asia* is good enough,' said Bashir with unexpected firmness.

Clara said, '*Stella Asiatica* is very chic, but Bashir has a point. A bit pretentious, maybe?'

Djamila pouted. She obviously liked to get her own way. 'But we are aiming rather up-market, aren't we Bashir?'

A couple of days later, it was Ghulam Ali's turn to visit. He brought a present for Clara, a dainty little painted papier-mâché box.

'Is made by sister's son in Kashmir. So much problem there now; peoples very sad, not doing carvings or paintings.' His brown eyes were melancholy.

Brendan could tell Clara liked him immediately, just as he had. He didn't stay long because he had to go back to the Tandoori and start preparing the evening's meals.

'I come again,' he promised Clara. 'Next time I bring pictures of *Lady of Shalott*. More time to talk then about family.' He went off shuffling down the path in his down-at-heel shoes, burdened with worries.

Spring had begun promisingly that year. An early Easter and a warm couple of weeks in mid-April had lulled everyone into believing that the mild weather would continue. It broke on Friday night. All night long it rained and didn't let up for a minute.

The next morning, Saturday, the day of the protest march and the SCOM meeting, Brendan parted his bedroom curtains and looked out on a swollen canal, the water swirling and eddying by. Outraged ducks swam past, looking half drowned in the volume of water. Relentlessly, the rain drummed away on the wooden roof, the bank a sea of mud.

About a million things still needed doing before the procession was due to set off at nine. The ponies had to be rounded up at dawn; the carriage dressed and decorated. The phone never stopped ringing and people kept arriving.

Commander Halsey put his head through the door.

'See you at the Town Hall. Twelve hundred hours sharp,' he barked.

Polly and Clara rushed around in a state of frantic activity tying bunches of flowers and artistically draping ribbon all over the carriage and ponies. They were soaking wet, their faces streaming under their souwesters.

Brendan had been looking forward to this day. Once the hullabaloo was over, he was determined to carry on with his own plans. Perhaps a petition to Downing Street, certainly a meeting with Nyree Dawn Dipper.

Ramzana appeared, carrying an oversized black umbrella. Bashir and Ghulam Ali followed. All three were in their national dress – a long shirt with tails and baggy trousers – but Ramzana was the most exotically attired.

Over his shirt he had on a velvet waistcoat embroidered with silver thread and on his head was a curly-haired grey astrakhan cap.

At two minutes to nine, Loveleen's silver-grey Golf braked sharply in front of the boat and she stepped out. She was wearing an extravagantly sequinned peacock-blue salwar suit – a long, flared tunic over baggy trousers tightly cuffed at the ankles. Will helped her to unload the banners and placards.

Brendan nudged Ramzana. 'Thinks she's going to a ball or something. She'll freeze in that outfit.'

He read the banners and placards as they were lifted out of the car for Loveleen. 'Fair Play for Political Prisoners', 'Prisoners Without Trial', 'Support Prisoners Without Friends', 'Rough Justice Isn't Just'.

'What's that mean?' he asked Ramzana.

Ramzana tried to explain. 'I think it means that it isn't fair. I know Just means fairness.'

Polly, Clara, Loveleen, Ramzana and Ghulam Ali climbed into the carriage. Will (in knee breeches and frock coat), Bashir and Brendan were to lead the ponies. Loveleen handed Ramzana his placard which read, 'Papa I Miss You'.

Reporters and photographers and TV cameramen all jostled one another, cursing the downpour and trying to get shots of the carriage as it set off. As soon as they arrived at the bottom of the High Street, they found quite a large number of people waiting to join the procession. There was one group from Sisters All and a smaller group from the Asian Cultural Forum, besides a number of friends and acquaintances whom Brendan recognized. There was Mr Khan and his fat son from the newspaper shop, the cooks from the Kashmiri Tandoori, James loping along with his habitual scowl on

his face, and other boat people. The procession swelled
in numbers as they made their way to the town centre.
Then the pelting rain subsided, leaving behind a light
drizzle.

Perched up in the carriage, Ramzana had a good
view, even though the hood was up. He looked at
his grandfather sitting opposite him, his hands tightly
grasping his old knees, a tense worried expression on
his face.

'Dada,' he called.

'*Beta?*'

'Nothing . . . ' he turned his face away, so Dada
wouldn't see the tears he could feel coming into his
eyes. Memories of those days when they had all been
so happy together came into his mind. He didn't want
to think about his mother. That wasn't any good; she
was never going to come back. But he couldn't help
wondering if she could see them all, wherever she was.
Him and Dada, whom she had loved, and Bashir. Safer
to think of his father. If only he could hear from him. If
only he was safe. He thought, 'Can he see the sky from
his prison cell? Will he get the letter I wrote last week,
all about the canal and the boat and the ponies and my
friends?'

The ponies clopped along peacefully. It was extremely
agreeable sitting in the carriage in the middle of a huge
crowd of people who were all on your side. The buzz of
conversation and good-natured laughter filled the air;
Sisters All sang 'We Shall Overcome' with great fervour.
Brendan looked back and caught Ramzana's eye and
they both grinned. They were just coming up to the
Shopping Arcade when Ramzana caught a glimpse of
an unmistakable head of carrot-coloured hair among the
shoppers. Surely Simon Thripp hadn't come to town on

a Saturday morning to support the Prisoners Without Trial march?

Splat! came the answer. And again, something came flying through the air and hit the carriage. Splat! Splat! two more eggs found a target. Splat! another flew past his ear and caught Polly. It trickled down her arm, a mess of yellow egg and broken shell.

'Oh come *on*,' she wailed. 'What's going on?'

A chorus of alarm rippled backwards right to the tail end of the procession. People were panicking because it was impossible to see what had happened inside the carriage, as the hood was still up.

Will stopped the ponies and calmed them. They had sensed the tension in the atmosphere. The sudden halt of the carriage caught everyone unawares. 'Ooh,' the cry travelled down the length of the crowd.

'It's a bomb!' yelled a very tall, dreadlocked Sister.

'Ooh,' went everyone again. They all milled around in a confused state, not knowing what to do. The nice, peaceful, orderly march was about to break up.

Will turned to the crowd, furious and red-faced. 'Don't be so daft!' he shouted. 'It's only eggs. Nothing to be frightened about!'

'Oh,' went the crowd in relief.

Meanwhile Ramzana had jumped out of the carriage and dodged his way through the Saturday shoppers to where he had seen Simon go. He thought he saw the back of Tariq's head in the crowd but then he was gone, lost in the mass of pedestrians. He chased them as fast as he could, but it was no use. There were too many obstacles in the way. Infuriatingly slow strollers, mums with triplets and courting couples who couldn't be parted to make room as he tried to work his way through them. He gave up and returned to the carriage.

'That was Simon and Tariq!' he shouted to Brendan. He panted, 'It was definitely them throwing eggs, but I've lost them.'

'Criminal hooligans,' said Will, disgusted. 'I'll go and see that little puppy's father after this, I will. Never mind now. We can't worry about them, there's no time.' They were at the Buttercross.

Commander Halsey saw this as a good chance to get some free publicity for SCOM. He weaved his way through the crowd handing out 'Wildlife Hates Exhaust' and 'Save the Meadow' placards and persuading people to hold them up for the benefit of the TV cameras.

S.P. Padgaonker C.B.E. began his speech. He was a busy little man, quite bursting with a sense of his own importance. He had one of those bald heads with a few strands of hair specially grown long so they could be trained over his baldness. Before he started speaking he spent ages twiddling with the mike and adjusting its height to suit his own.

'Friends,' he intoned with the air of a man fulfilling a serious destiny. 'Friends, I am most heartened to see this *tremendous* commitment on your part to *justice* and Human *Rights*.'

Pompous twerp, thought Brendan down below. Couldn't Loveleen have picked someone better than him?

Padgaonker continued. 'We are here today to *remember* our friend Abdul Karim Butt, who with so many others is a prisoner in his own country. Not charged with any crime,' he wagged his index finger, 'and not *even* allowed to plead his case.' His voice became shriller. 'Not *even* allowed contact with his family. His young son,' and suddenly he made a grab for Ramzana, 'is here with us today. This *poor child*,' he indicated Ramzana, 'fatherless

69

and motherless, wondering every waking hour whether his father is being starved, beaten or tortured.' He let his voice now drop like a Shakespearean actor and swivelled Ramzana round so everyone could see him better.

'And now this young man . . . what's your name?' he whispered audibly. 'Ah yes, Ramzana, is going to say a few words.' He pushed him towards the mike.

Ramzana's face was a study in panic. He had gone bright red. He could feel a rash of heat prickling his forehead. 'Oh, no,' he groaned inwardly. No one had said anything to him about giving a speech. What was he supposed to say? He gulped, blinked rapidly and said 'Ummmm . . .'

Brendan watching from a few yards away clenched his fists till his palms started to hurt. Go on, he urged. Go on Ramzana, you can do it. Start talking now, or you'll never say anything. Go on Ramzana.

The crowd waited, their faces turned expectantly. Ramzana was aware of a sea of faces, all blurred. Then he saw Brendan's face and his encouraging expression and started speaking into the mike.

'My father loves our country,' he began hesitantly. 'He is a patriot. He would never do anything to cause harm to Kashmir or to any Kashmiri, Muslim or Hindu. I want my father to be free so we can go fishing in the lake again.'

Tumultuous applause broke out. Brendan saw Ghulam Ali take out his handkerchief and blow his nose. The speeches went on for a bit after that, but the camera bulbs were popping all around Ramzana. Brendan felt terribly proud of him and gave Bashir a victory salute. When the meeting was over and the V.I.P.s had departed in their black limousines, Loveleen Tikoo tripped over to where

Ramzana was being fussed over by Will, Polly and Clara.

She put her arms on his shoulders and kissed him on both cheeks. 'You wonderful, wonderful boy,' she breathed. 'You were the star of the show. You'll be on the News tonight and I want you to know *you've made my day*!'

Brendan exchanged glances with Clara and they both grinned. Loveleen Tikoo making goo-goo eyes at Ramzana!

8

'You wonderful boy,' Brendan said with mock rapture. 'Come on wonder boy, we've got to get down to serious work.'

They were in the restaurant, trying to decide whether it was best to write a letter to Nyree Dawn Dipper or to telephone her.

The SCOM meeting in the Town Hall had gone well too. It was a full house and stirring speeches were made by committee members. The Appeal was read out and everyone signed yet another petition.

Now they had to wait for a verdict from the Department of the Environment.

'Brendan said, 'We ought to go to Downing Street anyway.'

'Remember, we said we'd wait until the result of the Appeal? It's going to cost a packet going to London and back and Will and Clara are sure to find out,' Ramzana cautioned.

'We could take the milk train early in the morning and miss school that day.' Brendan's original plan didn't feel quite as appropriate anymore.

A few minutes later he was dialling Nyree's number. 'What do I say?' he suddenly panicked.

'Don't worry, you'll think of something.'

The phone rang eight times. Brendan was about to put it down, when it was answered by a self-assured young voice. 'Nyree Dipper here.'

'Er . . . ' Brendan felt his palms going sweaty.

'Er, Brendan Dangerfield speaking. I read about you in the paper. How you won an award for saving the pond, I mean . . . ' he tailed off. Ramzana prodded him, 'Say you want to talk to her about it,' he whispered.

'Um, I'm trying to save a meadow in Stowbridge and I need some help. Can I come and see you to talk about it?'

A second's silence, then a brisk, 'I'll have to ask Mummy. Just hold on please.'

Mummy came on the line.

'Diana Dipper speaking,' came the adult but equally brisk voice. 'Can I help you?'

Brendan repeated what he had said to Nyree.

'We'd be glad to see you. When do you want to come?'

Brendan suggested next Saturday and they agreed on after lunch. She gave him elaborate instructions on how to get to where they lived. It was about an hour's journey by bus from Stowbridge.

On Saturday Brendan told Clara at breakfast that he was going to be out most of the day with Ramzana. Since she was used to his disappearing for hours on the Meadow, she didn't ask any questions. But Will said jovially, 'Off to Downing Street I expect.'

Luckily there was a bus to Great Grinling, from where it was a ten minute walk to Little Grinling. The bus got there at one o'clock, which meant they could be at the Dippers' by one-fifteen.

The Dippers' house was in an expensive new estate of 'executive' houses, each built in a different traditional style – there was mock Tudor, pseudo-Georgian, pebble and flint and even a thatched roof cottage. Nyree's was Regency, and was named 'Chimneys'.

'Posh,' Brendan observed, noting the expensive brass fittings on the door.

'Right on time,' said the chirpy-sounding girl who opened it. She ushered them into a gleaming kitchen with split-level cookers and lots of gadgets. Bunches of dried flowers and herbs dangled from hooks and they sat down under them at a scrubbed-pine table.

Nyree reminded Brendan of a chat show 'personality', rather like Esther Rantzen. He was familiar with the breed from watching Polly's TV. Words poured out effortlessly. She was poised and pert and very aware of her audience. She gestured with her hands, pulled funny faces and told stories against herself.

Flicking back waist-length blonde pigtails, she opened a fat scrapbook which was lying ready on one of the immaculate surfaces. It was crammed full of press-cuttings, photographs, pamphlets, fan letters and copies of petitions.

She pointed to a picture of a reedy pond.

'It all started as a joke. Mummy thought it would be fun if I got involved in Conservation. But it rather took over my life.' She sounded a trifle world-weary.

Apparently she'd started by writing to the local paper. She showed them the letter which ended, 'Yours concernedly, Nyree Dawn Dipper (aged 10).'

'Of course they had to print it. A letter from a ten-year-old is always newsworthy. Then they sent someone to interview me. After that the TV people rang and asked me to join a panel discussion. With a start like *that*,' there was a pause, 'it was quite easy to organize a campaign. You see, PR and publicity can give a great boost to a pressure group. But you also need lots of people who aren't afraid of making a terrible nuisance of themselves.'

Brendan exchanged a glance with Ramzana. She seemed to know all the ropes. He suddenly thought of Loveleen Tikoo. Nyree was a bit like her, too.

At this point in the conversation, Mrs Dipper walked in through the french windows, carrying a trug of freshly dug vegetables over her arm. She was brisk, like her daughter, and her delivery was emphatic.

'You have no idea,' she wagged a stick of rhubarb, 'of the *sheer slog* that went into this Hillcrest Pond Campaign. For a whole year I did nothing but drive around delivering notices, putting up posters, taking Nyree to meetings and interviews. Still, it was worth it in the end, wasn't it darling?' She looked fondly at her daughter. 'She's made a name for herself. Get the award, poppet, and show it to the boys.'

The award was a bronze cast of a baby seal.

'Sweet, isn't it? Now tell us about yourselves. I gather you've got problems.'

A jug of orange squash and a plate of chocolate biscuits was laid in front of them, and Mrs Dipper pulled a chair up to the table for herself.

While Brendan voiced his anxieties, Nyree sat with furrowed brow looking professionally concerned. 'Splendid,' she kept saying encouragingly in a middle-aged sort of way. 'Excellent,' she pronounced when he said the only solution was to do something dramatic.

She wasn't keen on the Downing Street idea.

'You'll never get through the security. Besides, who'll be there to notice that you've been? You want the media on your side, the local press and radio. Have you been interviewed yet?'

Patiently she went on. 'You see they'll love you –

the boy who wants to save the environment. They'll promote you as "A Plucky Fighter", or "Two Plucky Fighters".' She turned graciously to Ramzana. '"Two Plucky Fighters Go Their Own Way". It's a great head-line.'

Brendan looked at Ramzana. He hadn't thought of it like that. He began to realize that striking out on their own would mean an actual break from SCOM; and in a very public way. But perhaps Nyree was right. If they went about it the right way, then the fact that they were so young and battling against such mountainous odds might be to their advantage. They might get a hearing, where the adults had failed.

'What about the money for the barrister, if your Appeal fails?' Mrs Dipper asked. 'I know someone very eminent, Sir Barnaby Dalrymple-Hoskins. But his fees are very eminent as well. How is your committee going to get the money?'

Brendan muttered something about jumble sales and sponsored walks, which raised unbelieving laughter from mother and daughter. Diana Dipper clutched her head. 'You're not being serious?'

Nyree piped up, 'Mummy, shall we tell them about Cousin Howard?'

Mrs Dipper lifted her eyebrows and made her mouth into an O. 'Well done, Nyree.' She looked intently at the boys. 'My cousin Howard is a Member of Parliament. In this business, influence is everything. Dear Howard had a word with the Secretary of the Environment. I'm sure that's what did the trick.' It sounded like a circus act. She brought her face near Brendan, her glistening eye-shadow blue as a mallard's neck. Speaking in a stage whisper, each syllable extravagantly outlined, she urged him, 'Go and see your Member of Parliament. He won't be able to resist helping a youngster – and don't forget to tell the Press you're going to see him.'

Nyree had left the room. She now came back with a bulky file.

She said, 'I've just thought of something that might be useful.' She put down the file and extracted a piece of paper. 'When we were researching ammunition for our own case, Mummy dug this up in the Local History Library.' She gave Brendan the piece of paper to read. Ramzana leaned over to look as well. To save Brendan the embarrassment of stumbling through it in his usual laborious fashion, he read it out.

'"Right of Property Act 1925. Members of the Public shall, subject as hereinafter provided have Right of Access for air and exercise to any land which is a metropolitan common . . . provided that such rights of access shall not include any right to draw or drive upon the land any carriage, cart, caravan, truck or any other vehicle . . . "' He read it again, more slowly in order to make sense of the formal language. He looked at Nyree and Mrs Dipper, light dawning on his face.

'This means no one can drive a car over common land, either. Our Meadow's common land. That means Frank Thripp shouldn't be allowed to build a road, because if he does he'll be breaking the law!'

'That's right,' chorused the Dippers.

Mrs Dipper said, 'It means you have a very sound legal basis on which to argue your case – apart from a very good ecological one. This act has obviously been conveniently overlooked. That's what you can do – bring it to the notice of the powers-that-be while the Appeal is being considered.'

9

They had nearly an hour to wait before the bus left Great Grinling for Stowbridge. It was raining from a streaky, lint-coloured sky. They perched on an uncomfortable bench inside the bus-shelter and talked about what they should do next.

'I've got hunger-sickness in a big way.' Brendan clutched his stomach which felt as though it was sticking to his spine. He'd noticed before that excitement made him feel either very hungry, or very sick.

Ramzana rummaged in the pocket of his anorak and brought out a squashed half-bar of chocolate which they shared.

'First,' said Brendan ticking off a mental list, 'we've got to see our MP. Second, we've got to show him that Right of Property Act.' Nyree had photocopied the crucial document from her file on the Dippers' small photocopier. 'Third,' he finished chewing, 'we've got to get this done before they hear scom's Appeal.'

'Why don't we just tell Will about the Act,' Ramzana said in his reasonable way, 'then he can send it on to where the Appeal's gone . . . the Department of the Environment?'

Brendan dropped his gaze to the dirty floor, littered with cigarette butts and Spearmint wrappers. It took a while before he could pull his thoughts into a pattern that made sense; they were skittering in his brain like leaves in the wind.

He wanted to save his Meadow. It was as if he'd made a sacred vow. He owed it to the Meadow and everything that lived in it; to the place he loved, the place that had given him so much and was so much a part of him. Brendan knew it would mean real work but he desperately wanted to make the effort himself. It wasn't right, to hand the responsibility over to someone else. And he wanted to prove something to Will. He couldn't work out exactly what that might be; something to do with showing him that he wasn't daft, that he had ideas that could work.

All this rushed through his mind. He looked up from the dirty floor and said, 'No, let's do it by ourselves. Remember what Nyree's mum said? If we've got the MP behind us it might make all the difference. "In this business," he mimicked Mrs Dipper, "influence is everything".'

His mouth formed an exaggerated O and his eyes went into a frightful squint. Ramzana snorted with laughter.

'That Nyree's pretty smart,' he observed, a sliver of admiration creeping into his voice.

'Pretty, hmmm? Pretty *and* smart?' Brendan looked meaningfully at Ramzana. 'She's *awful*.' He pulled another face, sucking in his cheeks and letting his eyes go squinty again. 'Fallen for her, haven't you?'

'No I haven't,' said Ramzana huffily, hunching his shoulders inside his anorak.

Clara and Will were busy when he returned home. Will was going over his ledgers, his new NHS specs framed in pale plastic slipping down his nose. They gave him a benign look, quite out of keeping with his bizarre appearance; he looked like Mole in *The Wind in the Willows*.

Clara was stock-taking in her little exhibition room. Neither paid much attention to him; they both seemed preoccupied.

Over breakfast next morning, Brendan, trying not to sound too anxious, asked, 'When do we hear about the Appeal?'

'Let's see, today's the fourth of May. By the end of the month I should think,' Will replied.

Good. That gave them at least three weeks to carry out their plans. The most urgent thing was to get an appointment with the MP.

Ramzana had known his name. 'Dennis Underhill. He's always talking to the Asian shopkeepers about their problems. I think we'll find his address at the Community Centre near the Asian Cultural Forum.'

The Community Centre was housed in a converted Methodist chapel. The outside walls were painted with a mural of luridly coloured scenes of tropical life: women with baskets of bananas, palm trees and strange jungle animals. Two doors flanked the reception desk; one said SNOOKER, the other, CRECHE. Several people stood examining the notice board. All of them looked down in the dumps.

There was a bright yellow poster with the picture of a man with a broad grin on his face. 'Any Problems? Dennis Underhill, your MP will be pleased to see you at his surgery every Friday. 5–8 p.m. Please telephone for an appointment.' There was a number. Brendan took it down and they went out and sat down on the steps. 'Our problem, Mr Underhill, Sir, is that we can't wait till next Friday,' he said, addressing the garish coloured poster.

'We could phone him.'

'It's too complicated to explain over the telephone, Mr Underhill,' Brendan talked at the poster, 'we'd better write you a letter at the House of Commons.' He patted the sheet of paper and folded it before tucking it into his pocket.

He jumped up as the wheels of a double baby-buggy, constructed like a tank, nudged his left hip. The woman pushing it made clicking sounds of annoyance and marched inside, slamming the door. Brendan stuck his tongue out behind her back and flung himself down again.

'Come on, let's go and write this letter at my place,' said Ramzana.

A pale-blue Jaguar XJS, with the latest registration, was parked outside the Tandoori. The CLOSED sign was up, so Ramzana used his key to let themselves in. The restaurant looked spooky without any customers. As always, the tables were laid and waiting for their guests. Only one was occupied. Mr Rana sat next to the wall, so Brendan was able to get a good look at him, and Ghulam Ali sat opposite him.

Mr Rana was pudgy, as Ramzana had said. A roll of fat oozed over his shirt collar. His eyes were hidden behind black Mafia-type glasses. One hand shaped like a bunch of bananas covered with rings carried a cup of coffee to his thick lips, while the other bunch of bananas nursed a fat cigar. They were engaged in serious conversation. Ramzana's grandfather gestured placatingly, as though he were patting Tipoo and Sultan. Neither paid any attention to the boys as they went upstairs. Brendan could tell Ramzana was trying to eavesdrop.

81

'He's trying to get my Dada to do something for him,' he whispered. 'Something to do with Cousin Lubna in Kashmir – a wedding, something like that. Can't really tell what they're talking about.' He shrugged.

They sat on the bed to compose the letter. There were at least six attempts before it sounded right. Ramzana read out the final draft:

Dear Mr Underhill, MP
We are two boys who are fighting hard . . . '

Brendan interrupted. 'He might think we were fighting,' he objected. 'I mean the two of us . . . '

'Listen to what comes next,' Ramzana replied. 'Fighting hard *to* save a meadow. Not just fighting.'

'All right then,' agreed Brendan. It was of paramount importance that this first move should be flawless.

Ramzana went back to the beginning:

'We are two boys who are fighting hard to save a meadow from development. The Plan for a proper road has been accepted by the Council but the Stop Cars On the Meadow, scom, committee has appealed to the Department of the Environment who will give their decision at the end of May.

We have found this Act which says cars should not be allowed on Common land. We think you can help us by talking to the Minister because you meet him in Parliament every day. If the road is built, lots of rare and common birds will vanish from the Meadow. There are also rare plants like the Green Winged Orchid which no one else knows about as it might get stolen. Also, there are birds like green woodpeckers, larks,

Canada geese and nutcrackers from Norway in the summer.

We would like to meet you and tell you more. Please write back soon and tell us when to come.

Yours truly,
Brendan Dangerfield (11)
Ramzana Ali Butt (11½)

'I think we ought to say something like, "we were going to see the Prime Minister, but decided to come to you first."' Brendan put in.

'Why? What's the point? It'll only make him feel second best.'

'I disagree with you Mr Butt, and I hereby reserve the right to put forward . . . *my point of view.*'

Ramzana pushed him off the bed and they wrestled on the bare boards until they were helpless with laughter.

'Come on, let's finish it off. We've both got terrible writing and this paper's torn now.' Ramzana picked himself off the floor and dusted off his trousers.

'Will's got a typewriter. And proper paper,' said Brendan. 'I'll do it tomorrow after school, when he's at work.'

The letter took simply ages to type with one finger. Brendan messed up several sheets before it looked reasonable. Finally, it was finished, put inside an envelope and addressed to Dennis Underhill MP, Houses of Parliament, Westminster, London, and posted off that same evening.

Late that night, after he was in bed, Brendan heard someone knock at the door of the boat and then come inside. Whoever it was stayed for a long time. Brendan was groggy with sleep, but he could have sworn he heard what sounded like a dog snuffling and quietly whining.

83

10

Brendan had been so absorbed in his own affairs that he
hadn't been paying much attention to what was going on
at home. During that week, though, it started to register
that Clara and Will were distinctly edgy. Once or twice
he had walked into the living room and they had abruptly
stopped talking. They were also staying up until the early
hours of the morning.

One evening when he and Ramzana were sprawled all
over Polly's floor, watching the box and eating popcorn,
she said, 'Live Art Week's coming up soon. Do you know
if Clara's doing her usual thing of demonstrating canal
boat painting? I haven't seen her name on the list of
artists.'

'Don't know,' replied Brendan through a mouthful
of popcorn.

'I suppose she pulled out at the last minute . . . she's
got such a lot on her mind,' said Polly absently.

Live Art was a week-long event sponsored by the
Council every Spring. Artists and craftspeople in Stowbridge opened their studios to the public who came to
watch them painting, potting or making jewellery. Clara
demonstrated her cabbages and castles enamelware
painting and made a few sales that way. Brendan had
designed a poster for the annual event. 'CLARA STRONG.

PAINTED ENAMELWARE. Traditional canalware for sale in picturesque narrow boat.'

It was time for it to be displayed all over town, but Clara hadn't said anything about it to him.

He rolled over on his side to face Polly and looked at her for a few seconds. Polly could never keep anything to herself.

'Do you know if something's the matter? I mean, Mum's not upset about anything, is she?' He was really worried now, but tried not to let it show.

A blush crept over Polly's cheeks, which meant that something definitely was wrong. 'I don't know, Brendan. No, I'm sure everything's fine.' But it didn't ring true. Brendan made up his mind to ask Clara.

It couldn't be something to do with him. He cast his mind back. Apart from going to see Nyree Dipper and the letter to Dennis Underhill, he couldn't think of anything he'd done. Anyway those weren't the sort of things that would upset Will or Clara. He hadn't even been especially rude to Will lately. There hadn't been any scenes for quite a while. Still, you never knew with grown-ups. Will might have had enough of them. Maybe he was thinking of leaving. He wondered why the idea of Will going away didn't fill him with joy, or even relief. He must be getting used to him.

After the programme was over, he walked down the tow-path with Ramzana who was heading for Bow Bridge and home. He was wondering whether he should say anything to him about Will and Clara when Ramzana interrupted his thoughts.

'Something's wrong with Bashir.'

Brendan was scuffing a stone. He gave it a last kick. 'He's been really moody this last week, really bad tempered. You know Bashir, he never gets annoyed or upset. He won't tell me what's wrong, just keeps arguing with Dada. Do you think he and Djamila have broken up?'

'Just what I was thinking about Will and Clara,' confided Brendan, both alarmed and awed by the coincidence. 'It's the same at home. They're hardly talking these days and every time I come in they shut up.' Something else struck him. 'By the way, has Bashir been coming over to our boat late at night? I mean really late? I thought I heard his voice around one or two in the morning.'

'Dunno.' Ramzana shrugged. 'Could be. He always gets back late after seeing Djamila.'

Clara was on the phone when Brendan returned home from school the next day. She hurriedly turned her back.

'Yes, yes,' she was saying. 'Will's gone to see the solicitor. Look, can I call you back later? Can't talk now . . . bye.' She put the phone down.

'That was Granny,' she said a little too brightly. 'She's coming over at half-term as usual. Wants to know if you'd like to ask Ramzana to spend half term with the two of you in Dorset.'

Brendan didn't answer her question. Why couldn't she tell him what was bothering her? He knew, without the slightest doubt, there was something seriously wrong. But how could he help if Clara wasn't going to talk to him? He gulped hard and blurted out, 'Mum, can I ask you something? Are you and Will splitting up? You're both acting so strangely. Please tell me what's wrong?'

Clara burst out laughing. She came over and hugged him fiercely.

'Oh, Brendan, I'm sorry. Honestly, it's nothing like that. We *are* in the middle of a huge crisis, but it's nothing to do with us splitting up. Sit down and have some tea. I can see I'm going to have to tell you all about it.'

She made him some tea, cut some bread and butter and sat next to him tucking a strand of her long brown hair behind one ear. Reaching for the letter rack, she extracted an official-looking envelope and took out the contents.

'Listen,' she said.

'"Dear Sir/Madam,

It has been brought to our notice that you are making use of public land in a manner designed to exploit it for commercial purposes. The Council has received complaints about a carriage hire business which you operate from your narrowboat, *Fair Rosamund*. You are also advertising goods for sale and to order from the aforesaid *Fair Rosamund*. I am authorized to point out that you are in breach of planning regulations . . .
                    Terence Prosser
                    City Secretary and Solicitor"'

'I bet that was Frank Thripp who complained,' said Brendan.

Clara nodded. 'Who else? You see we're desperately worried, because if we can't run the businesses from here, where can we go? We can't afford to pay rent for stables and a studio. We had no idea we were doing anything wrong. Now we're running around getting legal advice and trying to make a case for ourselves. If the Council chucks us out we'll have to sell up and find somewhere else to live.'

Brendan felt a shock of alarm. Move away? Leave the boat? It was just too terrible to even think about. No good speculating on these gloomy possibilities with Clara right now. She was much too upset to offer him much comfort. Thank goodness she and Will were handling this together. He couldn't have carried that responsibility as well as worry about the Meadow.

Ramzana, too, soon had an explanation for Bashir's moodiness. He had been moving round listlessly for days now. Normally, it was as though the soles of his shoes were charged with an electric current; he danced rather than walked. His actions were impulsive, his movements quicksilver. 'I've got a great tape,' he'd announce bouncing in late at night, punching a cassette into his machine, moving a few steps, tossing his trousers over his shoulder and throwing himself on the floor energetically to do his press-ups.

Ramzana heard Bashir's footsteps dragging up the stairs. He was already in bed. He raised himself on one elbow and said quietly, 'Hi.' He didn't need to say any more. Bashir knew the greeting was more than a greeting. It included concern, sympathy and a question. He sat on the edge of his nephew's bed and gazed at him with tragic eyes, ringed with dark shadows.

'Right,' he spoke forcefully. 'I suppose I'll have to tell you.'

A terrible thought leaped like a djinn into Ramzana's mind. 'My father's dead.'

Bashir began talking. 'That son of an owl Rana was here the other day, do you remember? Well, he came with a marriage proposal for me. From his sister's daughter in Kashmir, Cousin Lubna. Dada wants me to marry her. A nice little traditional arranged marriage. It'll be good for the family, blah, blah, blah.' He looked wearily at Ramzana, searching him for sympathy. 'Rana said he'd cancel all our debts, raise our wages and buy us a proper house to live in.' A huge yawn took over his face. He waited for Ramzana to say something. 'Well, what do you say to that? Should I go along with Mr Pigswill Rana, or break Dada's heart by refusing?'

Ramzana looked at him steadily. It was obvious to him what Bashir should do. Tell Dada about Djamila and tell Rana where he got off. He didn't speak but his face said everything.

'I know, I know. Tell Dada about Djamila and very politely ask Rana to jump into the river. Thanks Chhota, that's just what I'm going to do tomorrow.'

He took off his waiter's dinner jacket and hung it on a wire coat hanger. 'Sorry I didn't tell you before. I've been out of my mind. You know I'd do almost anything to get poor old Father out of this mess here. But not quite everything.'

He rolled his socks into a ball and stuffed them into his shoes. 'I've been talking a lot to Clara. That is one hell of a nice lady. She really understands about me and Djamila and she's crazy about you. And Dada.' He turned round. 'Awful problems they're having at the moment. Shame, isn't it? Wish I could do something to help.'

Everyone, it seemed, was gripped by tension. Clara and Will looked harassed and tired all the time. Clara wasn't sleeping well. Brendan could hear them talking into the night and once or twice he heard her sobbing. He felt profoundly grateful that Will was with her, that they were in it together. He couldn't have been of much help by himself.

There was a perpetual round of phone calls and

visits to the solicitor and City Council offices. Officials came to *Fair Rosamund*, writing reports, scribbling busily on their clipboards with an air of professional detachment and bandying pleasantries. They came and went, faces buttoned up and exuding a kind of death-sentence calmness. They spoke in asides to each other, nodded significantly, then went away again.

Brendan and Ramzana waited in trepidation for an answer from Dennis Underhill. Ramzana stopped the postman every morning on his way to school to ask if there was a letter for him. No letter came.

'We should tell Will,' he kept advising Brendan. 'Let's tell him about that Act before they make up their minds against the Appeal.'

Brendan was adamant. 'Will's too busy. I don't think we should bother him with that now.' But he was becoming more and more uneasy and the more unsure he felt the more stubborn he became.

Ten days after the letter had gone there was still no reply from Dennis Underhill. It was the middle of May and the result of the Appeal was supposed to be known in only two weeks' time.

11

Rehearsals had begun for the Pageant. It was the annual showpiece of the Carswell Road Middle School Summer Fayre.

Stowbridge had seen a skirmish during the Civil War and King Charles, so it was said, had spent a couple of hours mustering his strength in *The Dog and Duck*. This little footnote in history, especially the battle between the Cavaliers and Roundheads, was the theme of a drama cobbled together by the Head of the school. Every few years it was taken out, dusted off, rewritten in racier language and presented before the Mayor, the Governors and parents. Mr Bulmer and Miss Trish Slee were in charge of the production.

There were no spoken parts, only a narrator; and Mr Bulmer was King Charles, while Miss Slee (who had very short cropped hair) played Oliver Cromwell. The children were hugely looking forward to the battle scenes and bloody corpses.

'As you've already proved your worth on TV you'd better be the Narrator,' Mr Bulmer told Ramzana. Simon and Tariq were Roundheads and Brendan was part of the Cavalier entourage. He was more than satisfied, since rehearsals cut out fifteen minutes of Mrs Titchbon time every Friday.

As they were clearing up after the first rehearsal, Mr Bulmer came up quietly to Ramzana and said, 'Any news of your father?' Loveleen Tikoo had phoned Bashir to say that representations were going to be made to Parliament. She had also received lots of messages in support of Abdul Karim.

Mr Bulmer patted Ramzana on the shoulder. He was a kind man and had been spotted in the Action Day march by Clara. 'Try not to worry,' he said. 'These things take a long time to get results.'

After school Brendan and Ramzana walked to Mr Khan's shop to buy sweets. A pound a week pocket money didn't go far so they always spent ages picking out a variety of the cheapest sort – gobstoppers, sherbert dibdabs, pear drops and acid pips.

'Can't wait to see Mr Bulmer in his wig,' said Brendan with relish. Rumour had it that Mrs Bulmer was as bald as a coot and that she owned a fine, long curly wig which would grace Mr Bulmer's pate on the day of the Pageant.

'I wonder if it's red,' he speculated, 'to match his bushy eyebrows.' They giggled helplessly at the vision of the overhanging eyebrows and curly wig.

While Brendan was choosing sweets, Ramzana was hurriedly sifting through the newspapers. He extracted *The Independent* from the pile and furtively leafed through it.

'Hey, you can't read the paper in here unless you're going to buy it,' Mr Khan's son shouted from behind the counter. He was a slow-moving, petulant looking young man, whose eyes missed nothing.

Ramzana paid for the paper and walked behind Brendan, almost completely obscured by it, shaking it out and re-folding it along its creases every few yards. He seemed to be searching for something.

'Trying to see if there's anything on Kashmir,' he muttered. He stopped and let out a whistle. 'Brendan, take a look at this.' He indicated a small headline.

'**MP in China** . . . Dennis Underhill, MP for Stowbridge, visited a bicycle factory in Szechuan province, China, yesterday. He is part of the five-member delegation on a trade mission to China. Mr Underhill said he hoped that the present import controls on Chinese-made bicycles to Britain would soon be lifted.'

'That's why we haven't heard from him,' exclaimed Brendan. 'Does it say when he's coming back to England?'

Ramzana brought his nose closer to the paper. 'Yes, here we are. "Mr Underhill, who left today for London, said . . . " That means he left yesterday.' He screwed up his eyes in an effort to work out the time-zone. 'China's further east, so travelling back to England he comes back west, so he must gain time. He'll be here today. He might even read our letter tomorrow when he goes back to his office.'

Ghulam Ali Butt was having tea with Clara. Despite the distracted air Clara had about her, Brendan could tell that she was making an effort with Ghulam Ali, trying hard to make him feel welcome and at home.

'Hello boys,' she called. 'Come and join us.'

She made room for Ramzana at the table. 'Your grandfather's been telling me about the *Lady of Shalott*.'

She pushed a photograph album across the table to Brendan. 'Have a look at these.' Pouring another cup of tea for Ghulam Ali she said, 'How I'd love to go there one day.'

He lifted his palms up prayerfully. '*Inshallah*, God's Will, maybe one day when problems finish you go stay with Abdul Karim on houseboat,' he intoned.

Brendan opened the album. The photographs were mostly black and white and the older ones, with pretty scalloped edges, were arranged at the beginning of the album. Pictures of Dal Lake showed water still as glass, mirroring the mountains beyond. 'It's *Dull* not *Dahl*,' said Ramzana. '*Dahl*'s what my grandfather cooks.'

The Lady of Shalott was enormous compared to *Fair Rosamund*. It had a carved and canopied verandah and sat high above the water. Ghulam Ali pointed to a yellowing photograph of an elderly man in a large white turban which sported a stiff fan-tail on top.

'My father,' he said proudly. 'Ali Abdullah Butt. He so fine cook, teach me all. *All*. Sponge cake, Christmas cake, ginger-bread, Queen of Puddings, caramel custard, trifle, roast goose, cutlets, apple sauce, apple crumble.' He had the same lilting way of speaking as Ramzana. The list sounded like a religious chant. 'He cook for British peoples.'

The original owner of *The Lady of Shalott* had been an English Colonel in the Indian Army, before the British left India.

Ghulam Ali explained. 'Maharajah Hari Singh – king of Kashmir – not wanting Kashmiri land belong anyone but Kashmiri peoples.' He placed his hand on his chest and closed his eyes. 'English peoples like Kashmir very, very much. So Maharajah say, "Okay, you can stay. Buy houseboat, not land. Enjoy."'

He turned the page for Brendan. 'Colonel Redmayne Sahib. Here, Mrs Redmayne. She so nice lady. Teach Ghulam Ali English. I young man then. Here, Master

Robin, Missybaba Sally.' Two children of about ten and twelve scowled at the camera.

'Do you know where the Redmaynes are now?' asked Clara.

'Colonel Sahib dead many years. Also Mrs Redmayne. Children big now. Forget Kashmir, forget Ghulam Ali. All world change. Children not listen to old peoples.' Now he was really upset. He looked away, his face strained with emotion. Then he got up and silently busied himself gathering his things into his cloth bag.

Ramzana knew what was troubling him. The night before Bashir had put his cards on the table. He had told Ghulam Ali about Djamila and flatly refused to have anything to do with Mr Rana's marriage proposal. There had been the most terrible row. Ramzana had gone up to his room, but he could hear Bashir and his father yelling at each other far into the night. Clara, too, knew what had gone on. She caught Ramzana's eye.

'Come Dada, I'll walk back with you,' he said taking his grandfather's arm to guide him out of the boat.

'He is such a good lad,' Clara said, picking up the plates and mugs and carrying them to the sink. 'I'm very fond of him. Did you know it's his birthday next week, on the 24th? What shall we get him for a present?'

Brendan pulled his hair and twisted it around his fingers. It helped him to concentrate.

'A surprise party. A picnic on the Meadow, that's what he'd like. Do you know Mum,' he confided, 'he spends all his pocket money on newspapers? He says *The Independent* and the *Guardian* give the most news about Kashmir, but they're very expensive, so he can only buy one every few days.'

'He could read them for nothing in the library,' Clara said. 'Tell him that, won't you?'

Clara wanted to involve Bashir and Djamila in the plot. 'I'll bake the cake,' she told them. 'A three layer devil's food cake.'

'You could make it like a cricket pitch,' said Brendan enthusiastically. 'A pavilion of chocolate finger biscuits and green icing for the grass.'

Djamila added, 'I know where to find some miniature cricketers, but you'll have to arrange them,' she told Brendan. 'I don't know the first thing about cricket.'

Bashir said he would get the drinks and the Cornetto ice-creams, which would stay frozen in an insulated box, and everyone gave Brendan money to buy the present. He knew just what it would be. He'd seen exactly the right thing for Ramzana – a game in the toy shop in the shopping arcade called Table Cricket.

> Sharpen your batting and bowling skills!
> Features automatic bowling.
> Ideal for indoors and out!
> Adjustable delivery action.
> Ideal for solo or team play.
> Complete with bat and six balls.'

The plan was for everyone, except Ramzana, to assemble at four o'clock on the Meadow. Somehow, Brendan had to lure Ramzana out there. Of course, no one was to breathe a word to him about what was going to happen.

Two days after Ramzana's birthday conference, a letter arrived at the Kashmir Tandoori addressed to Brendan and Ramzana. The envelope was long, cream coloured and made of thick, expensive paper. The letter-head said, 'House of Commons, London SW1 0AA'.

Underneath was a dark green logo of a portcullis with a crown over it.

Dear Brendan and Ramzana,

I have just read your letter of May 7th and am rushing off a hurried reply. I apologize for the delay in answering but I have been in China and only got back yesterday.

I shall be very interested to hear more about the Meadow from your point of view. I gather, from what you have said, that time is running short. I suggest, therefore, that we meet at the earliest opportunity. I shall be in Stowbridge on May 25th. Would you like to come to see me at the District Party Office in Steeple Street at 5 p.m. on that day?

With best wishes,
Dennis Underhill

It was beautifully typed and the signature was enormous, like skywriting.

12

Falling asleep, Brendan drifted gently on memories of the day; little pricks of realization and insight, the final private monologues before something turned off the switch of consciousness; the nightly comfort of nestling under his duvet and listening for the resident owl in the poplars opposite. Known and familiar routines had changed. Now questions kept repeating themselves, questions for which there were still no answers.

In the middle of a strange dream in which he was running away from soldiers with a huge blue, potted hydrangea in his arms, Brendan woke up with a distinct worry niggling like a worm behind his eyes.

'Of course! It's half-term next week. Ramzana and I are meant to be going to Granny's. But we can't, because we're seeing Dennis Underhill.'

The worm had worried his eyes wide open. Granny was, as usual, driving down to pick him up. It was great fun going to stay with her. Not only was she quite barmy, but she lived near the sea. For years, while Grandad was alive, she had led a pretty conventional existence and taught at the local primary school.

'A madly boring life, my dear. School, gardening, shopping, cooking and package holidays. Now I'm a free agent,' she would stress. 'I don't garden, I don't clean,

I don't cook – Marks & Spencer are doing very nicely – and I live for *me*.' She had started painting seriously and her paintings sold for hundreds of pounds. She had bought a motorbike and every now and then would disappear with her friend Esther to Italy or Spain or France, to paint and gather inspiration. Brendan had already warned Ramzana; half-term holidays with Granny were always unpredictable, but always eventful.

They could of course take a train to Dorset after their meeting. And it was Ramzana's birthday picnic the day before, so they couldn't go earlier as they had originally planned. Strange how Clara and Will and he had forgotten about half-term.

Luckily, Granny was so unpredictable herself that she didn't mind the change of plan, although Clara took her own memory lapse as sinister evidence of mental disorientation.

'Take the train on the morning of the 25th, after the party,' Will suggested.

'Uh . . . well, actually Ramzana can't travel on a Wednesday; it's . . . uh . . . considered unlucky in his family,' he invented.

On the morning of the 24th Brendan kept dashing into *Florian* to check the weather report on Polly's television. 'Fine and sunny earlier,' breezed the weatherman, 'with *some* chance of scattered showers in isolated patches in the south west.' By lunchtime the prediction had firmed to, 'mostly sunny with some cloud advancing from the west in the evening.'

At half-past three, the advance guard of Clara and Djamila went ahead to lay out the food and drink. Bashir followed, his arms wrapped round an ice-box full of Cornettos. Then came Ghulam Ali's diminutive figure pulled along by Tipoo and Sultan, one straining on his left arm the other on his right, so the three of them looked like the points of a triangle. After that awful row with Bashir he had reluctantly accepted his engagement to Djamila. Polly and Will soon appeared and Ginger and Jupiter, catching the whiff of food, trotted over from the far end of the Meadow to join them.

It had turned out to be a lovely afternoon, with the sun shining and only an occasional tatter of cloud floating across it. The hawthorn smelled sweet and cow parsley foamed in the ditches.

Brendan, meanwhile, was telling Ramzana some cock and bull story about needing to give the ponies stomach medicine in order to counter the effect of rich spring grass. He hurried him to the Meadow. They unlatched the barred gate and walked towards the small clump of trees behind which everyone was hidden.

All morning Ramzana had tried not to think about his birthday. Birthdays had not been made much of in Srinagar; usually he had been given money to buy what he wanted. But every year Susan had baked his favourite chocolate cake.

There was a chocolate cake with twelve candles sitting on the red and white cloth. There were Bashir, Djamila, and Dada, Will and Clara, Polly, and Ginger and Jupiter. Only Abdul Karim and Susan were missing.

Ramzana felt a shiver of pleasure and embarrassment as they all started singing Happy Birthday. Clara gave him the large package of Table Cricket. The cake was squidgy and chocolatey with a thick fudge icing, just like Susan used to make. There were cream cheese and pineapple sandwiches made with granary bread, mince pies which tasted even better in May than at Christmas, home-made cheese straws with a spicy tomato dip, banana bread thickly buttered and loads of ice-cream.

As soon as the eating and drinking were over, Bashir sprang up with a yell. 'Come on everyone, let's play *Pitoo*. It's a fab game we play at home. Ramzana and I will teach you.'

The two of them raced over to the gate, which was set into a broken drystone wall, and picked out handfuls of flat, shingle-like stones. From their collection they selected seven of the flattest, each measuring about fifteen by ten centimetres. These they laid one on top of the other in a neat layer.

The game was played with two teams. Bashir was captain of one and Ramzana captain of the other. They took turns to pick who they wanted; Will, Polly and Djamila were chosen by Bashir, and Brendan and Clara went to Ramzana's side. Ghulam Ali wouldn't play. He rubbed his shins and complained of his great age and said that he preferred to watch. Just then James was sighted in the distance trying out his new, Chinese mountain bike on the tussocks and hillocks of the Meadow, so Ramzana ran over to invite him to join his team. Now both teams were equal in number.

Bashir always carried an old tennis ball in his pocket to throw for the dogs. He began the game by lobbing it at the stone cairn – the seven tiles, as the game is also called. The stones scattered in all directions. Bashir's team raced to retrieve the ball, passing it from one to the other as they ran, as the rules forbade any player from running with the ball. Their aim was to try and hit one of Ramzana's team while they were trying to re-assemble the stones into the original pile. They, of course, hectically dodged all the while they were picking up the stones and rebuilding the cairn.

Clara was the first to be hit and had to drop out. James went next, but Brendan and Ramzana, yelling warnings and dodging like mad managed to rebuild the pile.

It was fast and furious and depended on teamwork and lightning reflexes. After five games they stopped, puffed out by the exertion, and collapsed on the grass. Ramzana's team won three games out of the five.

'There's a special prize for the Captain,' announced Bashir. With a dramatic flourish, he took an envelope out of his jacket pocket and gave it to Ramzana. Ramzana opened it and extracted a sheet of paper, which looked to the others like a letter. He read it through quickly and let out a great whoop of joy.

'It's a letter from my dad!' Holding it aloft, he ran to Bashir and hugged him ecstatically, jumping up and down with excitement. 'Dada, look! It's a letter from Dad!'

Pandemonium broke out in the party as everyone shouting with happiness crowded round Ramzana to thump him on his back and demand details.

He read it out:

'Dear Ramzana, Bashir and respected Father,

First of all, I am well. I have been in prison for four months now, but I am being quite well treated. In December I had fever and bronchitis, but a doctor gave me medicine. I cannot say very much except that I am to be allowed a lawyer and to make a plea for my release.

Please do not worry too much about me. As Allah knows, I am innocent. I hope I shall be allowed to leave once the trial is over. Bashir, your efforts on my behalf have been successful. Allah is a witness to your love for me.

102

Son, I think of you every day and miss you more than words can say. Your letter reached me. I am happy you have made friends and settled in your new school. Work hard at your studies so I can always be proud of you. Say hello to your friend Brendan from me.

Father, try not to worry too much, though I know you cannot help that. I am very happy that Bashir and Ramzana are there to look after you. Keep praying for me. I am sure I will see you all soon.

Your loving son,
Abdul Karim Butt.'

A hush fell on the company when Ramzana finished reading the letter.

It was Djamila who broke the awed silence. She said softly, 'The best birthday present you could ever have had.'

Will asked Bashir, 'How long have you known about this letter?'

'Only since this morning,' he replied, the broadest of smiles on his face. 'Loveleen brought it to the restaurant at about eleven.'

Ramzana couldn't keep still. He walked around, hugging the letter to his chest, reading it over and over again. He carefully folded it and put it away underneath his shirt. He felt very tired. A cloud covered the sinking sun. The poplars near the river had turned a bronzey pink and a cuckoo was still calling from somewhere.

13

'Sure you've got that Act that Nyree copied for us?'
Ramzana whispered. Clara and Will were in the next
cabin and Brendan was packing his school rucksack in
preparation for the meeting with Dennis Underhill in
the afternoon.

'I've put it inside one of my notebooks,' he whispered back. The four notebooks of his drawings and
paintings, Nyree's paper, and bits and bobs from the
scom campaign were safely stowed away.

'Brendan, come in here for a sec,' Will's voice pen-
etrated the wooden wall of the cabin. 'I've just thought
of a present to take to your granny.' He had the smug
look of someone with an unbeatable idea. 'Fishermen's
handwarmers.'

'Absolutely ace,' acknowledged Brendan. 'She can use
them when she goes landscape painting. She's always
complaining about freezing fingers.'

'Very reasonable too,' said Will. 'Less than £5, I
think. You can pick them up at The Compleat Angler
near Bow Bridge.'

Fishermen's handwarmers consisted of a small, flat,
velvet-covered box, no bigger than a spectacle case.
The inside was lined with reflective zinc and carried
two small sticks of charcoal, which when lit burned

very slowly, heating the zinc chamber, and spread their warmth to the velvet cover. When your fingers felt cold, you gripped the little velvet box like a miniature hot water bottle.

'That's really strange,' Ramzana said when they had made the purchase. 'We have something like this in Kashmir. In cold weather people fill small baskets called *kangris* with burning charcoal and carry them under their woollen caftans.'

They were on their way to meet Dennis Underhill. The District Office was located between the railway station and the industrial part of the canal that ran between the Thornbridge Brewery and some defunct factories. No green trees or suburban gardens softened the murky waters in this part of town. The canal stagnated in a sluggish flow of industrial waste, here and there brightened by a gipsy sycamore sapling or a vigorous buddleia bush somehow thriving in thrifty soil.

Next to a cavernous warehouse was a small brick building with a brass plate that said DISTRICT OFFICE and a handwritten notice that said WALK UP. They pushed open the door and walked upstairs on treads covered with gritty lino which led into a lobby. There was a noticeboard and another door with a sign, PLEASE ENTER.

Exchanging nervous looks they obeyed the request and gingerly opened the door into Dennis Underhill's room. A woman was working at a computer just inside the door.

Dennis Underhill turned away from his own computer and stood up behind his desk. 'Ah, the two campaigners,' he said effusively, motioning them to sit down.

'I wonder, Laura, if you could bring us some tea,'

he asked the woman pleasantly. 'And some chocolate biscuits?'

He was an enormous man, in height as well as girth, and looked much older than his photograph on the yellow poster.

'Well . . . ' he began, 'shall we get down to business?' He stared at Ramzana for a minute or two. 'Your face seems very familiar. Where have I seen you before?' He rubbed his chin. 'Of course, you spoke on television during that Human Rights campaign about a month ago, wasn't it? You know Loveleen Tikoo? So do I. She's a terrific girl. Tremendous energy. I believe she's trying to get some help for your father.' He looked sympathetically at Ramzana.

It was a good beginning. Dennis Underhill was feeling warm and benevolent. The boys relaxed a little.

He switched his attention to Brendan. 'Tell me, why have you written to *me*? I mean, if the City Planning Office has already decided that the road is acceptable, then what do you think *I* can do about it?'

Brendan caught a glimpse of their letter which lay on top of the pile of papers on his desk. He reached into his rucksack, brought out the file and notebooks and handed the photocopy of the Act to the MP.

'The Planning people didn't know about this. Or, at least, they didn't bring it up. You see, if they build the road, they'll be breaking the law.'

Dennis Underhill skimmed through the paper. 'Hmm . . . very interesting . . . but let me get this straight, why didn't your SCOM organization forward this to the Department along with the Appeal?'

This was the tricky part. There was a long pause. Brendan's palms began to sweat. How to explain the story of the SCOM campaign, how laid-back the committee

106

were, his impatience with their methods, his resolve to take direct action without telling the others and Frank Thripp's crooked dealings with the Council?

Ramzana spoke first. 'You see, the man who wants the road built is the landlord of *The Dog and Duck*. His name's Frank Thripp and he knows loads of people on the Council. He invites them to his pub and gives them free drinks and parties, so they're mainly on his side. He wants more business, that's why he put in the application for the road. But none of them care about the Meadow or the wildlife and plants . . .'

Brendan chipped in, 'The SCOM committee are much too nice. They're polite and *democratic* and they haven't been pushy enough.' He remembered Mrs Dipper. 'We couldn't get an effective pressure group together, and then Ramzana and I met this girl who told us about this Act. So we thought we ought to do something about it ourselves. We thought if *you* told the Department of the Environment they'd listen to you and get the Appeal turned in our favour. We've brought all the papers with us.' He gave his notebooks and the file to Dennis Underhill. 'These are my own records. That's what the Meadow's all about.'

The MP opened a notebook and examined it, leafing through it in a leisurely way. Laura brought in the tea and the chocolate biscuits and gave them a cup each.

Dennis Underhill put on his tortoise-shell frame glasses and looked intently at Brendan's paintings.

'These are terribly good,' he said. 'Do you mean to say you've actually got the Green Winged Orchid in your Meadow?' It was one of Brendan's best watercolours which he had done the summer before. It had taken a lot of experimenting before he'd got the exact shade of mauve. He remembered having tried scarlet and Prussian blue, crimson lake and cobalt blue, then vermilion and ultramarine until he'd captured the delicate pinky purple shade of the flower.

Dennis Underhill was looking at his bird pictures now. He said with regret, 'I've never, ever, seen a nutcracker. Last Autumn, someone phoned me from Essex to say there were two of them in his copse. He said I should hurry over before they moved on. But as luck would have it, I had an all night sitting at the House so I couldn't go.'

It hit Brendan like a bolt of lightning that the MP was spending all that time looking at his notebooks because he was a nature lover himself. Otherwise why would people be ringing him from the other end of the country to tell him about the nutcracker – a rare visitor to the British Isles?

It was a fantastic piece of luck that they should be dealing with a person who happened to be particularly interested in the very thing that they were concerned about.

He spent a good half an hour reading through the scom papers and looking at the notebooks. He scribbled some notes on a pad and pushed it to one side.

'Now,' he said at last. 'This Act that you've brought with you *has* actually been mentioned in passing by the scom committee.' He went through the file and took out a copy of the Appeal. 'Here it is. Right at the end. They probably didn't think it was a strong enough case.'

Brendan and Ramzana exchanged glances. They must have missed the reference to the Act in the convoluted language, so formal and so difficult to understand, of the Appeal. Why hadn't the scom committee highlighted it?

Brendan's heart fell with disappointment. So this

wasn't going to be the big coup he and Ramzana had intended. Ramzana's eyebrows went up and down in sympathy.

Dennis Underhill went on speaking. 'Strange how the City Council have chosen to ignore this piece of legislation. What the Council say is that the track is already a motorable road because the landlord of the *Dog and Duck* gets deliveries and mail. Tell me,' he looked intently at them. 'Is it really motorable? Is the pub at the end of the road, or off to one side?'

Brendan frowned. He couldn't see what the MP was getting at. He said, 'The pub's a good four hundred yards off the track. You have to go down a narrow path to get to it.'

'Where does the road lead to?'

'Nowhere. It ends at the bridge across the river.'

'Then it is *not* a motorable road. It doesn't go anywhere. But I'll have to check that. I once dealt with a very similar case. In other words, the road is not a road, it's a dead end. If we concentrate on this *and* emphasize the 1925 Act we'll have a good case.

'You said the Appeal's due to be heard any day now,' he said, clearing his throat. From a man of his size, it sounded like an elephant trumpeting. He walked to the window and looked out, his hands in his pockets. Then he turned round and said, 'It's going to be difficult.' He sat down again.

'I'm going to get a lawyer to look at this in some detail. We may have something here. If the track isn't motorable, it cannot be re-classified as a road.'

The boys sighed with relief. For a while it had seemed that their efforts might have been in vain.

'I don't want to seem to be using any pressure. But,' the MP said, gesturing at the notebooks, 'I am *most* impressed with your interest and your concern. And *if* scom win their Appeal, I'm sure it'll largely be due to your initiative in pursuing the case, and coming to me.'

Brendan's throat felt dry. One of his legs had gone to sleep. He prayed, 'Please let him help.'

'I'll see what I can do,' said Dennis Underhill standing up, indicating that their time was up. 'I'm seeing the Secretary of State tomorrow anyway. No promises, mind, but I'll see if he can do something.' He shook their hands, ushered them to the door and waved goodbye.

They clattered downstairs and began their walk home alongside the canal.

'Whew,' said Brendan wiping his brow with his hand. 'That was hard work. Have you any money for a drink? I'm parched.' Then he realized that in his excitement he had left his notebooks and papers in the office. He ran back upstairs and knocked on the door. The MP was getting ready to leave, his briefcase in his hand, but he was turning the pages of Brendan's notebook. He gave them to him and said, 'You're a very good artist. Keep at it, you'll go far one day.'

Brendan left, feeling almost dizzy with pride and relief that their mission was over at last.

'Well?' he looked questioningly at Ramzana, who was striding along in silence and hadn't voiced any opinion so far.

Ramzana bent down to send a stone skimming on the surface of the water. Brendan wasn't sure whether he spoke with real or feigned admiration. 'They're so clever. Politicians, I mean. I think he's going to help us, but not because he thinks we're wonderful, or because he's dying to save the Meadow.'

'Why would he bother otherwise?'

'It's his job. It'll make a nice story in the papers and make him look good, and then he'll get more votes. It's just like that in Kashmir. Politicians only want votes so they can hang on to power.'

Brendan felt a little disappointed. 'I thought he was okay. He liked us didn't he?'

'Oh, sure, but it suits him to like us. I bet he isn't always friendly and helpful. If it doesn't help him in some way, he won't go out of his way to help either.' Brendan was conscious that Ramzana knew a great deal more than he did about how the world operated. He wished he could still believe in Dennis Underhill's kind heart. Maybe Ramzana was being rather too cynical he thought.

14

Staying with Granny was a welcome break from the heady events of the past weeks. Brendan and Ramzana went walking on the coastal path, climbed rocks, slept late, ate lots of frozen pizzas and chicken Kiev. Nothing much happened. Granny locked herself into the bathroom once and couldn't get out, so they had to call the Fire Brigade who rescued her through the window. Apart from that nothing dramatic took place.

On Friday, back at school, Mrs Titchbon leaned over Brendan's shoulder to inspect his cursive writing. He had attempted to put some flair into his practice, modelling it on Dennis Underhill's flamboyant signature.

'This won't do at all, dear,' she clucked. 'Much too large and those loopy loops are quite unnecessary.' She bent a little closer. 'I've just written a press release. I talked to your stepfather earlier. The verdict on the Appeal's been delayed, goodness knows why. But my brother Neil, you know the one who works in the Town Hall, says that's a very good sign; otherwise they would have turned it down without any problems.'

Brendan met her gaze. Her big teeth were as yellow as corn-on-the-cob. She nodded encouragingly. 'We may hear some good news soon.'

There was a phone call for Brendan on Sunday evening. Someone called Linda Phelan from the *Stowbridge Herald*. She said she wanted an interview with him and Ramzana. She'd had a tip-off from someone in the Town Hall that the two of them had been to see Dennis Underhill about the SCOM Appeal. She wondered if they'd mind having a little chat with her. Brendan looked round. Thank goodness Clara and Will were outside and couldn't hear.

'It won't take long,' promised Linda Phelan. 'I just want an update on what's happening.'

This was too much. Their direct action seemed to be taking on a life of its own. It looked as though their secret was about to be splashed all over the press. When he told Ramzana about it afterwards, he had said that probably Dennis Underhill himself had told Linda Phelan about their visit. 'Don't you see? He steps in and saves the Meadow. It'll be good for his image.'

Linda Phelan was waiting. He hedged. 'It's a bit early for a story isn't it?' To his relief she seemed to agree.

'But if the SCOM Appeal is successful,' she said, adding coyly, 'which my informant tells me it's going to be, then will you give me an exclusive story? With pictures?'

On Wednesday, just as he was leaving for school, an official-looking envelope arrived addressed to The Chairman, Stop Cars on the Meadow Campaign, *Fair Rosamund*, Nixey's Yard, Stowbridge. Will opened it to find that the Department of the Environment had agreed that the Appeal should override the previous decision taken by the Planning Office.

'Don't you see?' Will was practically hysterical. 'It means we've won!' He read: '"After careful consideration, etc, etc, etc, the Department of the Environment has decided that the path across the Meadow should not be made into a permanent, tarred thoroughway and that vehicular traffic should not be allowed on it, etc, etc, etc . . ."'

Brendan felt a twinge of the old irritation. Little did he know, the smug nincompoop. He wanted there and then to tell him the true state of the matter, but it was getting late. He'd do it after school.

Will was still raving as he left. 'This calls for the mother of all celebrations! I am getting on the blower to tell everyone to put the champagne on ice!'

Brendan stopped briefly at Polly's to let her know and then ran to school, feeling that he was treading on air.

Ramzana was walking down Carswell Road, so he told him the news and they punched each other happily.

'We did it Bren, we saw it through. We're the champions!'

They arrived at the school gate and the first thing they saw was a man with a camera round his neck and a woman who could only have been Linda Phelan with a notepad and pen and purposeful air to her. They were questioning children coming in, asking if they happened to be Brendan or Ramzana.

'Oh, no,' groaned Brendan.

Someone pointed out the two, 'There they are.' Linda Phelan and the photographer made a beeline for them.

A party was in progress when Brendan and Ramzana arrived back from school that afternoon. Polly, Will, Clara and Commander Halsey were all sounding rather merry with a bottle of champagne on the table. Will emptied his glass. 'Well boys, shall we carry the glad tidings to our great and good friend Frank Thripp?' He hiccupped.

There was a knock on the door. Brendan went to answer it. 'Hello Brendan,' a voice familiar to Ramzana boomed outside. 'Thought I'd pop over and see if you'd heard the good news. Can I come in for a minute?' And Dennis Underhill, stooping low to enter the boat, stood there in front of the gathering. He introduced himself and shook hands all round.

Will, who was looking totally bewildered, asked, 'How do you know Brendan?'

'Oh, I'm on nodding terms with him and Ramzana,' chortled the MP. 'Haven't they told you yet?'

Clara and Polly and Commander Halsey were all looking perplexed. Will burst out with, 'Told us what?'

'Well, the scom campaign might never have achieved its aims if these two extremely resourceful lads hadn't been to see me. They presented your case, got me involved and Bingo! with the help of some top legal advice I got the job done. By a whisker, mind you. The Appeal was about to be considered on the day my legal friends got their arguments sorted out. The timing must have been controlled by someone up there. You've a lot to thank these two boys for. I'd be very, very proud of them if I were you.'

The headline above a picture of a sheepish-looking Brendan and Ramzana said:

YOUNG NATURALISTS RESCUE OPERATION
Two youngsters from Carswell Road Middle School are the heroes of the scom campaign. Brendan Dangerfield (11) and Ramzana Ali Butt (12) backed by local MP, Dennis Underhill, have been able

to convince the Department of the Environment against all other expert advice that the proposed road across the Meadow will cause untold damage to wildlife and the environment.

The boy heroes discovered an obscure law which states that vehicular traffic is never to be allowed on common land. They then contacted Dennis Underhill for help with their cause.

Mr Underhill, well known for his espousal of green issues, told the *Herald*, "I have been most impressed by their courage and initiative. These outstanding youngsters should be the toast of the town. They are a credit to their school and their parents."

Brendan and Ramzana were the centre of attention for a whole week; pats on the back, smiles on the street, 'Saw your picture in the paper', radio interview, phonecalls, cards and letters of congratulations.

Nyree sent a tasteful card with a message. 'Well done! If you would like to come and spend the day with me, I could take you around Hillcrest Pond and we could compare notes.'

Mrs Dipper had added a PS, 'So glad everything has worked out for you. Told you!'

Ramzana secretly noted that the envelope was addressed to *Ramzana* and Brendan.

'The point is, will success go to your head? Might end up making you even more headstrong . . . ha ha.' Will looked quickly to see if Brendan had taken offence. 'Seriously Brendan, how are you coping with all this publicity?'

'Everyone on this planet is going to be famous for fifteen minutes once in their lifetime,' Clara said.

'Looks like we made it.' Brendan said happily.

Preparations were afoot for the greatest celebration ever seen in the neighbourhood of the canal. It was to be a composite celebration for the SCOM victory, for Brendan and Ramzana's gamble which had come off, for the successful contact with Ramzana's father and because, after all their anxiety, Will and Clara had found a viable and affordable site for their business.

Tom Wilson, Will's boss, had offered them a large garage and store-room in his builder's yard. The carriage would live in the garage and they could run an office from the store-room. All at a very reasonable rent. Now there was no need to leave their canal home and start life again in a new environment.

The party started with fireworks. Thornbridge Best and champagne flowed in equal measure. Cartloads of biryani and kebabs arrived from the Kashmir Tandoori, where the CLOSED sign was up for the evening so that everyone could join in. After that came music and dancing.

Ranzana and Brendan sat on the cabin roof watching the grown-ups cavorting down below and tried to stop themselves from laughing at the sight of James performing on the penny whistle, his disdainful features screwed up in an agony of concentration.

'Let's do something awful to Simon Thripp and Tariq,' Brendan said idly. 'A leaky bottle of ink in their games kit?'

'No, leave it, they'll know it was us. They'll be in trouble soon enough when they get to James' class in the Autumn.'

Ramzana fumbled in his pocket. 'I've found out who The Lady of Shalott was,' he said, unfolding a piece of

117

paper. 'The librarian told me it's a poem.' He recited a little self-consciously,

> *'On either side the river lie*
> *Long fields of barley and of rye*
> *That clothe the wold and meet the sky;*
> *And through the field the road runs by*
>   *To many tower'd Camelot;*
> *And up and down the people go,*
> *Gazing where the lilies blow*
> *Round an island there below,*
>   *The island of Shalott.'*

He glanced up to see if Brendan was interested, then continued:

> *'Willows whiten, aspens quiver,*
> *Little breezes dusk and shiver*
> *Through the wave that runs forever*
> *By the island in the river*
>   *Flowing down to Camelot.*
> *Four grey walls and four grey towers,*
> *Overlook a space of flowers,*
> *And the silent isle embowers*
>   *The Lady of Shalott.'*

'I haven't copied down any more,' he said. 'It's very long and really sad. She dies in the end.'

Brendan said, 'It's got Camelot, hasn't it? King Arthur and his knights and Queen Guinevere.'

James had finished his recital. There was a babble of voices below as some of her friends tried to persuade Clara to sing. They heard her protesting. Then Will came inside and fetched her guitar. She agreed at last and arranging her skirt around her, sat down on the canal side to tune her guitar. Brendan hadn't heard her sing for months. She sang, *Spencer the Rover*, a ballad which he loved and which brought him out in goose-bumps whenever he heard it. It was the story of a wanderer who leaves home to seek his fortune and after many misadventures comes back again.

His children came around him with their prittle-
*   prattling stories,*
With their prittle-prattling stories to drive care away.
And now they're united like birds of one feather,
Like bees in a hive, contented they be.

So now he's a living, in his cottage so contented,
With ivy and roses growing all round the door,
He's as happy as though he's got thousands of riches,
Contented he'll be and go roving no more.

Spencer the Rover had returned home to his children. Ramzana, sitting with his knees drawn up to his chin, was thinking, 'I wonder when my dad will come home from prison. The houseboat will need seeing to. But at least I know he's alive and safe and that there's a chance that he *will* be free one day.'

The song had ended and Clara's fingers plucked the last, minor cadence of the refrain. When she sang Brendan felt she lost herself somewhere in the singing, so that her spirit wandered and embraced the spirit of the song. Her long, straight hair fell on her shoulders and her head was tilted in the sad and haunting attitude he had seen in the Guinevere picture in the museum. But he knew that Clara was basically not sad, only a small part of her. Just like a small part of him would always be apart from other people, a little private. But a larger part of him was connected; to Clara, to Will, to Ramzana, to Polly, to Ghulam Ali, to Bashir, to Abdul

Karim; even to Simon and Tariq in some strange way.

Suddenly, he saw another connection. Guinevere, who had lived in Camelot, who reminded him of his mother, must have been connected to that lady on the island, the Lady of Shalott. It was comforting, really, to know that things linked up somewhere and in some form, even if you couldn't always see it.

Join the RED FOX Reader's Club

The Red Fox Reader's Club is for readers of all ages. All you have to do is ask your local bookseller or librarian for a Red Fox Reader's Club card. As an official Red Fox Reader you only have to borrow or buy eight Red Fox books in order to qualify for your own Red Fox Reader's Clubpack – full of exciting surprises! If you have any difficulty obtaining a Red Fox Reader's Club card please write to: Random House Children's Books Marketing Department, 20 Vauxhall Bridge Road, London SW1V 2SA.